I0586686

THREESOME

BRIAN W. SMITH
KEITH THOMAS WALKER

KEITHWALKERBOOKS

Publishing Company
KeithWalkerBooks, Inc.
P.O. Box 331585
Fort Worth, TX 76163

For information write
KeithWalkerBooks, Inc.
P.O. Box 331585
Fort Worth, TX 76163

ISBN-13 DIGIT: 978-0-9967505-7-8
ISBN-10 DIGIT: 0996750576
Library of Congress Control Number: 2017910743
Manufactured in the United States of America

Second Edition

Visit us at www.keithwalkerbooks.com

MORE BOOKS BY BRIAN W. SMITH

The S.W.A.P. Game
Mama's Lies - Daddy's Pain
Donna's Dilemma
Nina's Got a Secret
Larry's Got a Secret Too
Beater
Deadbeat
If These Trees Could Talk
Differences
Amnesia
Hoarder
Quagmire
Glass Houses
The Delusion of Inclusion

SLEEPY CARTER MYSTERY SERIES

The Audubon Park Murder
A Murder in the Quarters
Passé Blanc

SHORT STORIES

Close to Home
The Perfect Lie
Lagniappe
My Husband's Love Child

Visit authorbrianwsmith.com for information about these and upcoming titles from Brian W. Smith

MORE BOOKS BY
KEITH THOMAS WALKER

Fixin' Tyrone
How to Kill Your Husband
A Good Dude
Riding the Corporate Ladder
The Finley Sisters' Oath of Romance
Blow by Blow
Jewell and the Dapper Dan
Harlot
Plan C (And More KWB Shorts)
Dripping Chocolate
The Realest Ever
Jackson Memorial
Sleeping With the Strangler
Life After
Blood for Isaiah
Brick House
Brick House 2
One on One
Brick House 3
Jackson Memorial 2
Backslide

NOVELLAS

Might be Bi Part One
Harder
Primal Part One
The Realest Christmas Ever
Hotline Fling

POETRY COLLECTION

BRIAN W SMITH   KEITH THOMAS WALKER

Poor Righteous Poet

FINLEY HIGH SERIES

Prom Night at Finley High
Fast Girls at Finley High
Bullies at Finley High

Visit keithwalkerbooks.com for information about these and
upcoming titles from KeithWalkerBooks

ACKNOWLEDGMENTS (BWS)

First and foremost, I would like to thank God. I would also like to thank my family, friends, avid readers, and the book clubs that have spent their hard earned dollars on my books. Your constant encouragement and support throughout my career has served as my literary jumper cables whenever I've wanted to stop writing.

ACKNOWLEDGMENTS (KTW)

Of course I would like to thank God, first and foremost, for giving me the creativity and drive to pursue my dreams and the understanding that I am nothing without Him. I would like to thank my mother for always pushing me to be the best I can be. I would like to thank Janae Hafford for being the best advisor, supporter and little sister a brother could ever have.

I would also like to thank (in no particular order) Beulah Neveu, Deloris Harper, Denise Fizer, Michele Halsey Hallahan, Priscilla C. Johnson, Kim Tanner, Tia Kelly, Edwina Putney, Melissa Carter, Cathy Atchison, Lanita Irvin, Ramona Weathersbee, Cynthia Antoinette Taylor, Jason Owens, Ramona Brown, Sharon Blount, BRAB Book Club, and Uncle Steven Thomas, one love. I'd like to thank everyone who purchased and enjoyed one of my books. Everything I do has always been to please you. I know there are folks who mean the world to me that I'm failing to mention. I apologize ahead of time. Rest assured I'm grateful for everything you've done for me!

INTRODUCTION

Brian W. Smith and Keith Thomas Walker are rising stars in the literary world. Their combined resumes comprise more than 40 novels. Several of their novels have made the Amazon, Dallas Morning News, Target, and Black Expressions best sellers lists. Brian and Keith have won and been nominated for numerous awards to include "Male Author of the Year" and "Book of the Year" from several reputable literary organizations.

In THREESOME, these two talented writers join forces in a unique way to bring readers a steamy thriller.

Brian gets this jaw dropping novel started by introducing the reader to the protagonist and antagonist in Chapter 1. Keith ratchets up the drama in Chapter 2. From that point on, the authors continue this alternating by chapter style (Brian wrote the odd number chapters and Keith wrote the even number chapters) until the explosive ending. What makes THREESOME unique is that neither author knew what the other author was going to write. Their goal was to create an organic story; free from the shackles of excessive outlining. Each chapter is an untarnished reflection of each author's imagination. In one month, these two wordsmiths completed a story that is nothing short of amazing, and proves that they are literary forces to be reckoned with.

Now that you've been given the "behind the scenes" peek into how THREESOME was created, you should find a quiet spot and get ready to experience the literary ride of your life.

CHAPTER ONE

"Please don't, Corey."

The plea seeped from the full lips of the caramel colored beauty sprawled on top of the conference table and ping-ponged off the walls of the narrow room.

"Be quiet," Corey ordered.

"You can do anything to me..." the woman squirmed and arched her back as if she was giving birth to the rest of her sentence, "anything but that. You know what that does to me."

"Shut up!" Corey replied. The adrenaline rush made his husky voice sound an octave higher. He dipped his hips and plunged deeper inside of her.

"Oooh," she purred.

Beads of sweat dotted Corey's forehead. His nostrils flared and flapped like a bed sheet struggling to remain tethered to a clothes line during a stiff breeze.

A smirk appeared right before Corey continued his taunting. "I told you I can do what I want, didn't I?"

"Yes, Corey. Do what you want to me, baby."

"Shhhh," Corey hissed and placed an index finger over his mouth for what seemed like a minute. His neck craned in the direction of the thick door that led from the hallway into the conference room. His stroke was frozen. His heart rate slowed to a snail's pace.

The woman's chest rose and fell as if her heart was struggling to burst through. She managed to open her eyes long enough to catch a glimpse of Corey's signal to be quiet. She muted her passion by biting down on her bottom lip until Corey gave the "all clear" signal.

Corey's "all clear" came in the form of rougher sex. He gripped both of her ankles and positioned them around her ears. Without warning he smacked her perfectly sculpted butt. The impact of the blow sent her body into a state of confusion. Tremors rippled throughout her extremities. The response she wanted to unleash was being tugged on by two opposing feelings: joy and pain. Gritted teeth kept her words trapped inside of her mouth; hovering just above her tongue and being stretched to the point that they were reduced to nothing more than a pitiful sound when finally unleashed.

"Uhhh," was the only response she could offer.

"Now, I'm gon' ask you again. Are you gon' give me what I want?"

"Yes," she conceded.

Corey released her ankles. The woman's muscular legs recoiled until her feet rested on his chest. Corey smiled. Her nipples grew harder. His eyes zeroed in on the orange toenail polish. Lust swirled around them like a tornado.

Corey could feel his manhood pulsate the moment the tips of her manicured toes touched his lips. "Give 'em to me," he demanded and opened his mouth like a draw bridge.

The anticipation was killing his companion. Her breathing became more labored when spurts of his breath flirted with the tips of her toes. Resistance was futile. She shoved her toes inside of his warm mouth.

Corey closed his mouth and moaned while he sucked her toes. His thumbs massaged the bottom of her feet while his dick plunged deeper. His stroke was so fast and consistent that moisture seeped from her body and lathered his crotch.

"You gon' make me cum," she whispered. Her eyes rolled backward. "Shit, baby!" Her fist slammed on the slick table. "I...I'm..."

"Umm, hmmm," Corey mumbled and released his vice-like grip on her toes.

"I'm cuuummmin'!"

That catatonic state is where she remained until her limbs relaxed and she started to flop on the table like a fish out of water. Corey watched with amusement—and so did the housekeepers who spied through the partially open door on the other side of the room.

"I've gotta get cleaned up," Corey said and backed away breathing like he'd just run a marathon. He used his forearm to wipe the sweat on his forehead. "You need to get out of here too." Just like that, he was done with her. He headed down a long corridor that connected the conference room to his office with a condom still draping his limp dick.

The woman struggled to recover from her full body orgasm. She managed to sit upright and slide her wet butt off of the table.

Where are my panties? she wondered, seconds before spotting the white laced front thong dangling from the leaf of a rubber tree plant located in the closest corner. Her stretch-knit sundress with the botanical print and shoulder baring neckline rested on the chair at the head of the conference table.

"Giiirrrl, you'd better get yourself together."

After a deep breath and exaggerated exhale, she scooped up her panties, sundress, and sandals and walked—naked—toward Corey's office.

Corey exited his personal bathroom just as she arrived in his office.

"Do you mind if I get cleaned up in your bathroom?"

"Be my guest pretty lady."

Corey gestured in the direction of his office bathroom like a game show host pointing out a new prize. He smacked her butt as she walked past.

"Ouch!"

"I'm sorry," Corey said and chuckled, "that ass was calling me."

"You'd better hurry up and get home before Rene starts calling you," she replied.

"I'll head home once you finish your *hoe bath*."

A middle finger was her non-verbal reply.

Corey Grand, President and CEO of Grand Security Services, stood behind his leather, nail head trimmed swivel desk chair, and stared out the massive floor to ceiling office window that overlooked Freeport Parkway. He'd moved his company's headquarters into the swank building located in Irving, Texas one year earlier—much to the chagrin of his wife, Rene.

'In order to be big, you've gotta think big,' Corey proclaimed.

Rene Grand, Corey's drop dead gorgeous wife who possessed a MBA from Wharton, strongly disagreed. Her response to his "think big" philosophy was, *'Baby, I understand what you are saying, but sometimes less is more. Having a strong EBITA is what will enable Grand Security to not only become big, but remain big.'*

Corey, a college dropout, felt his ability to hustle was more valuable than any business school strategies his wife learned at that hoity-toity college she attended. The floor he stood on and the window he gazed out of at that very moment—despite Rene's protest—was proof that doing things his way was the best way.

"Okay, I'm going to get out of here," the woman said, looking as sexy as she did when she first arrived at his office.

Corey turned and sized his mistress up. "I had fun."

"So did I."

"Until next time?"

She walked over and kissed him on the lips. "Only if you promise to suck my toes again."

"You try to keep those toes from me, but they always end up in my mouth. You like that freaky shit, don't you?"

"You know I do," she whispered.

"If you promise to keep those feet manicured and soft I'll keep doing my part."

"I promise." She gave him a peck on the lips. "You'd better get home. I don't want you to get into trouble."

"Shit...you're right," Corey mumbled while looking at his watch. "You leave first. I'll wait a few minutes and leave after you."

Rene sat on the couch with her laptop braced on her thighs while Corey Jr. positioned his six-year-old frame in front of the massive sixty-inch television and recited lines from his favorite movie, *Cars*.

"He can't beat you, Lightning McQueen!" CJ shouted.

"CJ, don't talk with your mouth full."

Without moving his lower extremities, the child turned his upper body one hundred eighty degrees to look at his mother. "I'm watching, *Cars*, mama," he replied, with ramen noodles slithering out of his mouth.

"I know you are, sweetie. But mommy doesn't like when you talk with your mouth full."

"Mama—"

"CJ, do I need to tell daddy what you are doing?" Rene asked, peering over the wire framed eyeglasses perched on the bridge of her nose.

"Noooooo, mama," CJ whined and shook his head.

"Well, do as I say."

CJ nodded and looked at the television. He remained in that trance for thirty more minutes. It had become his routine: the animated movie, *Cars,* sitting Indian style in front of the television; and stuffing his face with ramen noodles.

Rene, who served as an online college professor when she wasn't homeschooling young CJ, finished grading her last paper. "Finally!" She closed the laptop with authority, removed her glasses, and rubbed her bloodshot eyes.

"Shhh, mama," CJ said. "You too loud."

"Says the child who acts like the television has to be blasting for him to hear it," Rene mumbled. "I want you to sit here and finish watching your movie, okay."

"Umm hmm."

"What are you supposed to say, CJ?"

"Yes, ma'am."

"That's my baby." Rene moved in from behind, clasped CJ's chubby cheeks, forced his head to aim skyward, and kissed him on the forehead. "I've got to get ready."

"Where you goin' mama?"

"Daddy and I are going out on a date."

"What's that?"

"We're going to get something to eat."

"Can I come?"

"No, CJ. Tonight is mommy and daddy's night to go eat dinner. But, I have a surprise for you."

"What? Some candy?"

"No," Rene said and chuckled. "Ms. Jennifer is coming to babysit you. Don't you like Ms. Jennifer?"

CJ nodded. "She's pretty."

Rene shook her head. "Is she prettier than mama?"

CJ shook his head.

"Good answer." Rene went into her bedroom. *It's four minutes to six. Corey, where are you?* She grabbed her cell phone and dialed Corey's number.

"Hello!" Corey tried to speak louder than the roar of the V-10 engine growling under the hood of his Audi R8.

"Baby, it's almost six and we have a seven o'clock reservation at Oceanaire."

"I know, bae. I had a lot of shit piled on my desk that I didn't get to yesterday. Honestly, I focus better when no one is in the office." Corey changed the topic. "Who's babysitting CJ and what time is she supposed to come?"

"Jennifer is watching CJ tonight. I asked her to get here around six-thirty."

"Who?"

"Jennifer. You know, Greg and Tracey Foster's daughter—the one who recently graduated from college. We used her to babysit last year when we went to the Super Bowl Party."

"Oh, yeah, I remember. Hold up, Greg and Tracy only live a few miles from us. It won't take fifteen minutes for us to make it to Oceanaire. You said the reservation is at seven so why would you have her come thirty minutes early? She's gonna charge us for time that we'll still be at home."

"Jennifer is in her twenties. You know that age group is notorious for being on CP time."

'True," Corey agreed.

"I told her to be here a little earlier because I'm expecting her to be a little late."

"Good thinking. Well, if it'll make you feel better, I'm less than five minutes away from the house. Do me a favor and grab somethin' out of my closet for me to wear."

"Why? All you're going to do is tell me you want to wear something different and make your own selection."

"Am I that bad, bae?"

"You're worse."

"Touché," Corey said and laughed. "Well, like I said, I'll be home in a few."

"Good. I still need to hop in the shower, and I would prefer to do it when you're here so you can watch CJ."

"Where's Lil Man?"

"Where he always is—"

"Watching *Cars*."

"You know it."

"Okay, I'm a few streets away."

"Okay."

When Rene heard the garage door open she turned on the shower and stepped inside the steam filled capsule. Corey entered the house via the garage door that led into the laundry room which was connected to the kitchen. He smiled when he saw CJ staring at the television like a zombie.

"Where is my *Lil Man*?"

"Daddy!" CJ leapt to his feet and was in Corey's arms before he could put his keys on the counter.

Corey may have been a lot of things: cocky, flashy, a womanizer; mean at times; and even a little chauvinistic, but he could never be called an inattentive father. The bond he and young CJ shared was as deep as the ocean and as evident as the noses on their faces.

On a few occasions, Rene watched with envy as Corey and CJ doted over each other. Her efforts to illicit that type of unbridled joy from her baby boy often failed.

'I'm the only woman I know whose son came out the womb a "daddy's boy",' Rene would often say to friends and family; to which Corey routinely replied, 'You had nine months to connect with him. If you didn't do it that's a "you" problem not a "me" problem.'

Corey showered the child with kisses on his face and neck. CJ giggled like he was on an amusement park ride. Nearly five minutes passed before Corey put the boy down.

"Go finish watching your movie. Daddy's gotta get dressed."

"I wanna come with you, daddy," CJ whined and wrapped his tiny arms tighter around Corey's leg.

"I want you to come too, Lil Man," Corey whispered, "but mommy wants to hang out with daddy alone."

"Why?" CJ asked.

Corey shrugged. "I don't know, son. I guess it's a *woman* thing. They call it *date night.*

CJ's face scrunched.

"I know...that's corny, huh? You know some woman came up with that crap." Corey patted CJ's head. "You'll learn about *date night* when you get older. Now go watch your movie."

Corey went into his bedroom. When he opened the bathroom door it looked like London during the Jack the Ripper era. He squinted and tried to fan away the thick moisture clouds on the way to his closet.

"Baby, hurry up and take a shower," Rene said, as she exited the shower just as Corey walked past.

Even with limited visibility Corey could see the beads of water glistening on Rene's exposed chocolate shoulders and collarbone.

Corey grabbed at her towel.

"Stop playin', Corey, and get in the shower. I don't want to be late."

Corey quit the horseplay and walked inside a closet that looked like a men's clothing store. He ambled over to the left side of the room where his things were kept. Hard heel shoes, loafers, and sneakers rested on an eye-level high shelf that spanned the width of the wall. His suits hung high and his pants were underneath. Shirts of all colors were to the left and an assortment of neckties hung to the right. A thigh high glass encasement, where cuff links, bowties, and watches were kept, doubled as the peninsula that kept he and Rene on their respective sides.

After spending fifteen minutes trying to decide which shoe, belt, and watch combination to wear, he made his decision and walked back into the bedroom.

Rene allowed the towel to fall to the floor and revealed the most flawless chocolate skin known to man. Perky breasts, slanted eyes, and curvy thighs kept the California beauty looking twenty-seven even though she was three months away from leaving thirty-seven behind.

"Damn, baby," Corey said, as he watched her slither into a pair of jeans. "You think we have time to—"

Corey's advance was cut short by the doorbell chime.

"Stop right there!" Rene said and held up her hand. "That's Jennifer at the door." She pointed toward the bathroom. "You. Shower. Now."

"Alright, alright," Corey said and threw up his hands in surrender.

Rene took a moment to button her blouse and then went to answer the front door.

"Hey!" Rene greeted. "Girl, you're right on time. Come on in."

"Of course!" Jennifer countered and gave Rene a quick *church style* hug.

"I'm so happy you agreed to babysit for us. When I told CJ you were watching him tonight he lit up like a Christmas tree." Rene nodded in the direction of the living room. "He's in there." They moved from the long hardwood foyer and into the grand living room. "I think my baby has a crush on you."

"Aww, that's sweet," Jennifer replied.

"CJ, honey," Rene called out, "look who's here...Ms. Jennifer."

CJ glanced over his shoulder and smiled.

"I told you my baby has a crush on you."

"I wish I could get that kind of attention from someone my age," Jennifer said.

"Girl, stop it!" Rene said and waved dismissively. "You are gorgeous. With a face and body like that, I *know* you're not having a problem finding a man."

Jennifer shrugged. "I have a *friend*, but it ain't too serious."

"Nothin' wrong with having a little *fun* at your age," Rene said. "Ooh, I love this sundress. I really like the way it falls off your shoulders."

"Thank you. I got this at Nordstrom last week."

"It's really nice," Rene said and pointed at Jennifer's feet. "And that nail polish—it goes perfect with your outfit."

"Thank you," Jennifer said. "I'm not crazy about the color, but my *friend* loves it. He's got a toe fetish."

"Haaaaaaay!" Rene stretched the word to let Jennifer know they were on the same page. She offered Jennifer a high-five and whispered. "If the boo-thang loves the color then keep the damn color."

"I know that's right," Jennifer replied and moved toward CJ. "What'cha watchin', Lil Man?"

"Cars," CJ replied. "That's my favorite movie."

It's almost six-thirty. We need to get going, Rene thought as she glanced at the clock.

"While you two get reacquainted, I'm going to go check on the hubby to see if he's ready." Rene went into the bedroom and was pleased to see Corey drying himself off. "That was fast."

"I'm a dude, bae. All we need to do is wash our ass, crotch, and arm pits and we're ready."

"Gross," Rene said, while applying her lipstick. "Jennifer is in there with CJ. We can leave whenever you're ready."

Corey moved behind Rene and pressed his body against her butt. "You sure we don't have time for a quickie?"

"I'm positive." Rene turned around and kissed Corey on the lips. "Now get dressed so we can leave."

Ten minutes later they both exited the bedroom.

"We're about to leave," Rene announced. "CJ, come give mommy a hug."

CJ walked over and gave Rene a lazy hug.

"Hey, Jennifer," Corey said while Rene and CJ said goodbye. "Thanks for *coming* over."

"No problem," Jennifer replied with a wide smile. In a tone just above a whisper she said, "I love *coming* over here to see, Lil Man. I'll *come* whenever you ask me."

Rene snapped her fingers. "Your money. Let me go get it out of my purse—I just need to remember which purse I was carrying when I went to the ATM." Rene looked at Jennifer. "Girl, my memory is getting worse by the day."

Rene hadn't left the room three seconds before Corey and Jennifer were flirting with each other.

"Girl, you lookin' so good, I wanna hit it some more," Corey whispered and rubbed Jennifer's butt.

"You're lookin' good too," Jennifer said and winked. "I almost didn't make it."

"Why?"

"Because you zapped of all my energy earlier." She nudged him in the side. "I told you to leave my toes alone. You know that's my spot."

"I found it," Rene said holding a one-hundred-dollar bill in her hand. "I know you're only charging twenty-five an hour, but I want you to take this."

"Oh no, I can't."

"No, I insist," Rene said. "I called you at the last minute and you came through for me. I appreciate it."

"Come here, Lil Man," Corey said. "I want you to be good for Ms. Jennifer."

"Okay," CJ said.

"Go, go," Jennifer said. "Y'all gon' be late."

"Okay, okay," Rene said and headed toward the door. "We should be back around midnight."

"C'mon, Rene," Corey said, "you bugged me about getting ready and now you're gonna make us late."

"There is food in the fridge," Rene blurted out.

"Bye!" Jennifer said and flicked her wrist urging them to leave. "Me and my boyfriend here are going to be fine."

"Aww, sookie," Rene said, "sounds like my baby is giving "toe man" some competition."

Jennifer blushed and moved close enough so only Rene could hear her. "If yo' baby grows up and learns to do the things "toe man" can do with a pair of feet, you gon' need a shotgun to keep the women from stalking CJ."

Rene shook her head and lifted her hands like she was testifying. "Stop it! Stop it! You gon' make me grab some popcorn so I can hear more about this *friend* of yours."

Rene walked past Corey and made a beeline for her car, which was parked in the driveway. Corey looked back at Jennifer and winked before closing the door behind him.

Jennifer rested the back of her head on the front door after they left and closed her eyes. She remained in that spot for a few seconds and thought about their boardroom tryst. Her eyes opened and a smirk appeared as she glanced down at her toes and thought, *Girlfriend, I don't think you could handle the stuff I could tell you about "toe man."*

CHAPTER TWO

"How are things at work?" Rene asked.

Corey kept his eyes on the road as he piloted the car to the Oceanaire Restaurant in the Galleria. "Things are going very well," he boasted. "Did I tell you we secured the contract for the mall they're building in Houston?"

"No, you didn't. I knew you were waiting to hear back from them."

"We got the call a couple of days ago."

"That's great!" Rene exclaimed. "How in the world did you let something like that slip your mind?"

"Had a lot of projects on my desk this week. I thought I told you. Sorry."

"This should be a celebratory dinner tonight. Every time I think my admiration of you has peaked, you make me more proud."

A prideful smile parted Corey's lips. He reached to caress his wife's thigh. Rene placed a hand over his and smiled appreciatively.

He looked over at her and said, "You make me proud too."

"Really? And what have I done to gain your praise, Mr. Grand?"

"I'm proud of you for working the hell out of those jeans."

Rene laughed at that.

"If I knew you were gonna look this delectable tonight," Corey continued, "I would've canceled our reservation and found a bed and breakfast instead."

His caress heated her chest as much as his words did.

"We haven't done that in so long," she said, grinning. "I wouldn't have minded. But I don't think Jennifer would go for it."

"You think she's got something better to do?" Corey asked. "You told her we'd be out late?"

"Yeah. I told her we'd be back around midnight. But I wouldn't be surprised if she has plans that start that late, as pretty as she is."

Corey nodded, agreeing that their babysitter was very attractive, right down to her pretty, little toes. Memories of sucking them sent a pulse of electricity down his torso. It settled between his legs, just as his wife's hand moved in that direction.

"Hmmm. You really do want to skip dinner tonight," she noticed. She smiled as she stroked him slowly. "I'd be agreeable if you weren't taking me to my favorite restaurant. I've been looking forward to this all week."

"Spoil sport," Corey muttered.

"I'm sure CJ will be fast asleep when we get home," Rene offered. "We'll have all the time we need to make our own bed and breakfast."

"Cool. I can't wait. I'll be sure to eat some raw oysters tonight."

"Yeah, like you ever need help with your libido," she said with a smirk.

You are so right, Corey thought. *I've got enough loving to go around!* "Never hurts to be *more* potent," he told her.

"You'll never hear me complain about that," Rene agreed. She continued to caress his hardening member.

"Woman, you better stop, before I pull off this freeway and find a secluded area, like we used to do back in the day."

The thought of going down on him made Rene's mouth water, but she withdrew her hand and let him concentrate on driving.

Corey looked over at her again and shook his head slightly. "I knew you wasn't down."

"Oh, I'm down," she assured him. "But I'm also hungry."

He chuckled and his eyes returned to the road. "Spoil sport."

Corey pulled up to the valet at The Oceanaire and hopped out of the car with a cocky smile. He tossed the keys to the attendant as he went around to open the door for his wife. She took his hand and he helped her out of the car. Rene smiled brightly as she rose to her full height. Beneath the moonlight and the restaurant's bright marquee, her husband's bronze skin seemed to glow. Rene had always believed she married the finest man in Dallas. The fact that Corey had chosen her to tie the knot with delighted her to no end.

He wrapped a possessive arm around her waist and led her into the restaurant. The delectable aromas from the fine dining titillated her senses the moment they stepped inside.

"Mmmm. I love it here," she hummed.

"I know you do. I love bringing you here."

"Do you know what you're having?" she asked. "Wait, let me guess. The whole, steamed lobster with steak."

"You know me so well."

"And raw oysters, since you think your libido needs a little help tonight."

"I never said I needed help. The oysters are for *your* benefit."

"Then by all means, get a whole platter," Rene said and laughed.

"Good evening," the host said as they approached his station. He was in his early twenties, bright eyed and handsome.

"Good evening," Corey replied. "Reservation for Corey Grand."

The host looked down at his computer and then grabbed a couple of menus. "Yes, sir. Right this way."

"Corey Grand!"

Rene thought she was hearing an echo as their host led them through the crowded restaurant. Her eyes widened when she followed the voice to a table for two. Wayne Gregory, Corey's closest friend, sat with a beautiful vixen who had tons of caramel skin on display. Wayne rose to his feet as Corey turned towards him.

"Wayne! What are you doing here?"

Corey's smile was ear-to-ear as the men came together for a bro hug.

"Eating," Wayne said. "Same as you. You think you the only one who can afford to dine in a joint like this?"

Corey did not think that. While Wayne may not have been the CEO of the marketing firm he worked for, he was only a few notches down the totem pole.

"Nah, of course not," Corey said. "Just didn't know you had plans to come here tonight. You should've told me. We could've hooked up for a double-date."

"I don't think it's too late to pull that off," Wayne replied. "We just got here a few minutes ago. Haven't even ordered yet."

Corey looked past him to the pretty, young thing seated at his table. She smiled politely, but Corey could tell she was hoping he'd decline Wayne's offer. The dress she had on made it clear that she wanted *all* of Wayne's attention that night.

"Nah, I wouldn't want to intrude," Corey told his friend.

"Nonsense!" Wayne's bass-filled voice boomed, drawing more attention to the handsome men. "We would love to have you – unless you and Rene would prefer to be alone..."

He looked her way and said, "How are you doing, Mrs. Grand? You look lovely tonight."

He stepped to her and took her hand, bringing it to his mouth for a kiss.

Rene hoped Corey didn't notice how she nearly swooned like a southern belle. Wayne was 230 pounds of dark chocolate delight. His career was white collar, but he had the build of an NFL running back. His hair was styled in a crew cut. His eyes dark, his jawline rigid.

Despite his hand being large enough to completely swallow hers, Wayne's touch was soft. His lips on the back of her hand caused a field of goose bumps to sprout on Rene's forearm. She regained her composure quickly enough to respond without a noticeable gap in the conversation.

"I'm fine, Wayne. Thank you. And we would love to have dinner with you and your friend – if you're sure it wouldn't be an inconvenience..."

Rene looked at his date, who had remained mute. The woman maintained her smile as they locked eyes, but Rene could read her thoughts clearly:

Yes, that would be an inconvenience, thank you very much!

Get over yourself, hussy, Rene replied, also with her eyes. *You're not the first, second or third woman Wayne's been out with this year. Hell, you're not even the first one this summer!*

"Sabrina, you don't mind, do you?" Wayne asked, looking back at his new flavor of the month. "This is my friend Corey and his wife Rene. I've known them for years."

Sabrina was polite enough to say, "Oh, no. Not at all. The more the merrier."

"Great!" Wayne turned back to Corey and slapped him on the shoulder. "I guess it's settled then."

"Well, if you insist," Corey replied.

"I think it would be awesome," Rene chimed in. "We need to celebrate Corey's new contract anyway."

"You got a new contract?" Wayne asked, beaming.

"Yeah. It's kind of a big deal," Corey confirmed.

"That's great!" Wayne said. "Hey, can you move us to a bigger table?" he asked the host, "so we can celebrate with our friends?"

"Oh, well, it's um..." The man looked down at his notepad.

Wayne produced a fifty-dollar bill so smoothly, it looked like sleight of hand. He tucked it into the host's breast pocket, and suddenly the information on his notepad was invalid.

"Yes, sir. Right this way."

An hour later, the men were boisterous at their new table near the front of the restaurant. For appetizers, the group enjoyed spicy tuna and grilled octopus. For his main course, Corey went with the meal Rene predicted – with raw oysters on the side. The foursome was on their second bottle of wine, so the ladies didn't mind the men's banter. Rene watched Wayne across the table, growing increasingly impressed with his achievements, even though they were supposed to be celebrating Corey's new contract.

"No, you are not behind those stupid Mint Dentistry commercials!" Corey balked. "Every time I turn on the radio, the DJ's yucking it up with those assholes!"

Wayne laughed. "If you hear my commercials every time you turn on the radio, then I'm doing a good job."

Corey couldn't believe it. "You're really responsible for that?"

Wayne nodded. "I write those scripts personally."

Corey shook his head. "And it's working?"

"They're building a new office in Fort Worth and two more in Dallas as we speak," Wayne confirmed. "We're not supposed to invest in our clients' stocks, but I had to get in on theirs. I suggest you call your broker and do the same."

"Have you heard those commercials?" Corey asked his wife.

"All the time," Rene said. "I've been thinking about popping in to get my teeth cleaned. I heard they're offering free lipstick."

Corey laughed at that. "Baby, you've got enough makeup to be an Avon lady. I know you're not hurting for lipstick."

"No, but if it's free, might as well get more."

"*Exactly!*" Wayne said. "A tube of lipstick is nothing. But when people hear the word *free*, it messes with their head."

"They offer a free cleaning too," Rene recalled. "Everything on their commercial sounds free."

"That's how they get you," Wayne said knowingly. "Everything's free, till they tell you how many cavities you have. And best believe they're gonna find at least one tooth that needs a root canal. Maybe they'll yank it out altogether and talk you into an implant. That's where the real money is. No one wants a jacked up smile. I don't recommend you go there," he confided. "They make hundreds of dollars for every tube of lipstick they give out. It is a good investment, though."

"Thanks for the heads up," Rene said, looking him in the eyes. "But I don't know how they'd feel about you chasing away potential customers."

"I'd rather maintain our friendship than toss them another customer," Wayne said honestly. "They'll be alright. In fact, they're doing great."

"Thank you for your honesty."

Rene continued to smile at him. It didn't feel like she and Wayne maintained their gaze for too long, but maybe they did. She looked over at Corey when he cleared his throat and addressed the fourth person at the table.

"So Sabrina, where'd you hook up with this clown?" he asked Wayne's date.

"*Clown*?" If Wayne was offended by that, it didn't show. His smile remained megawatt. Rene thought his teeth were perfect. She wondered if he was a Mint Dentistry customer himself.

"I work at the Aura Lounge," Sabrina told them.

"Oh yeah? What do you do there?" Corey asked.

"She's a bartender," Wayne answered. "Sexiest thing in the place," he said, looking Sabrina's way. She gushed at the compliment. "Almost turned me into an alcoholic," Wayne joked. "The first time I saw her, I sat at the bar for hours, just to watch her mix drinks. Every time she'd squeeze a lime wedge, I'd think about how it would feel if she was squeezing my..."

Wayne looked back at his friends, as if he'd forgotten they were there.

"Sorry," he said with a grin. "Never mind."

"Squeezing your *what*?" Corey wanted to know. "You done went a little too far with that story to back out now!"

"No, I could never speak that way in front of Rene," Wayne said, locking eyes with her again.

Rene wanted to tell him she was as interested in the answer as her husband was, but she knew Corey wouldn't take too kindly to that. An embarrassed, amused smile brightened her features.

"He likes his nipples squeezed," Sabrina revealed.

Wayne shot her an annoyed look that spoke volumes about their relationship. Sabrina was clearly out-classed by the man she was dating. She may have been looking for something substantial, but Rene knew she was just another notch on Wayne's bedpost. One of many.

That opinion should've made Rene view Corey's running buddy unfavorably, but she didn't. Wayne was handsome, single and successful. As long as there was no ring on his finger, Rene thought he had a right to indulge in all the beauty the city had to offer.

"Your *nipples*?" Corey balked, a tad bit too loudly. "What kind of grown-ass man wants his nipples squeezed?"

Rene got a good laugh out of that. She knew the good food and strong wine coursing through her system had her feeling more jovial than usual.

"Ain't nothing wrong with exploring different erogenous zones," Wayne told his friend. "You, *of all people*, should know that."

Corey's mouth snapped closed, and he piped down instantly. His reaction went mostly unnoticed, but Rene regarded her husband curiously, wondering why Wayne's comment had that effect on him.

You of all people...?

Was that an inside joke? Rene didn't see how Wayne could know more about Corey's fetishes than she did.

"Anyway, I managed to get Sabrina's number before I got too twisted," Wayne told them.

"No, you didn't," she contradicted, laughing. "I had to call you an Uber."

"You only did that to find out my address," Wayne countered. "Once she found out what neighborhood I stayed in," he said to Rene and Corey, "she asked *me* for *my* number."

Sabrina continued to smile at him, rather than disagree with that.

Rene and Corey arrived home at a quarter after midnight. They were still in good spirits as they entered the kitchen from the garage. They quieted down, expecting their son to be asleep, but CJ rushed down the hallway with his babysitter quick on his heels.

"*Daddy!*" he squealed, totally oblivious to the fact that his mother longed for such unmitigated joy when she arrived home.

But such was the curse of a stay-at-home mom. Rene and CJ were together so much, he rarely built up enough yearning to actually miss her.

"Hey, buddy!" Corey knelt to give him a hug.

He looked over the boy's shoulder and noticed Jennifer heading their way. She looked as fresh as a springtime sunrise. Corey saw that she had taken her sandals off at some point in the night. Her beautiful toes sank into their plush carpet as if she was stepping on snow.

Corey's heart skipped a beat as he followed her toes up her legs, past her full thighs and slim waist, and finally to her face. She grinned at him and had the same bright smile when she acknowledged the woman of the house.

"Hey, Rene. I know you said you'd be here by midnight, but I didn't expect y'all to get back so soon."

"I appreciate you for helping us out," Rene replied. "I'd never take advantage by asking you to stay later than the time we agreed on."

"I would've been fine," Jennifer replied. "I don't have anything going on tonight."

"I thought maybe your boyfriend would want a little of your time," Rene said.

"Nope," Jennifer said with a smirk. "He's busy tonight." She looked down at CJ as Corey rose to his feet. "I swear I had CJ in bed," she explained. "I was in the den watching TV. He jumped up when he heard the garage open. This little rascal must've been faking sleep."

She rubbed the top of CJ's head affectionately. The boy looked up at her, beaming proudly.

Jennifer tried to give him a stern look, but then she laughed. "Aww, I can't stay mad at you. You're too doggone cute!"

"Don't let that cute face fool you," Rene warned her. "He'll try to get over on you, if you let him."

"No, I won't," CJ protested.

"Oh, well that's because you have a crush on Miss Jennifer," Rene replied.

The boy's eyes grew large. His cheeks reddened at the same pace. "*Mama!*"

He rushed from the room to hide his shame. The adults laughed as they watched him go.

"I shouldn't have said that," Rene told them. "It's true, but I shouldn't have said it in front of him. So, he didn't give you any trouble?" she asked Jennifer.

"Not at all," she replied. "You can call me over anytime. I'm glad I don't have any kids, but I certainly don't mind yours."

"Good," Rene said. "We'll keep that in mind."

"Well, let me go get my shoes, and I'll be on my way," Jennifer said. "I think I left them in the den."

"I need to get out of these heels," Rene complained. "Thanks again for coming."

The women embraced briefly before heading down the hallway.

A moment later, Jennifer found Corey alone in the front room. She didn't think he'd try anything as bold as he did before he and Rene left for the restaurant, but his eyes darkened as she neared him. Gone was the slightly inebriated smile he wore a minute ago when he embraced his son.

"Don't you ever take off your shoes in my house," he muttered.

Initially stunned, Jennifer looked back, to see if they were alone in the room. They were. She noticed a slight grin in the corner of Corey's mouth, and her tension eased. She stepped closer, until they were nearly chest to chest.

"Or what?" she asked, speaking as softly as him. "What if I do?"

The scent of her perfume was intoxicating. Her defiance was even more so. "I'll take you, right then and there," he threatened. "I don't care who sees."

"Yeah right," she said with a smirk. "I'll take my sandals off right now, and you won't do a goddamned thing."

"Oh, you got one coming for all this noise you're talking," Corey said, shaking his head. He reached to open the door for her. "Next time we're together, I'm gonna stuff something in that trash-talking mouth of yours."

"Promises, promises," Jennifer said as she walked past him.

Corey followed her onto the porch and reached for her hand, turning her back to him. He knew it was risky, but he couldn't help himself. He pulled her into his arms. Once there, his hands moved to her ass. He gripped both cheeks. Hard. Jennifer gasped, but the hug was over just as quickly as it began. Corey released her and backed away, moving a bit stiffly now.

Jennifer shook her head, grinning. "You are so bad."

"Actually, I'm *worse*," Corey said.

His dark eyes were piercing, causing her heart rate to kick up another notch.

"Remember what I said," he told her.

Corey had said so many outrageous things that night, Jennifer wasn't sure which one he was referring to. She didn't get a chance to ask, because at that moment another figure joined him in the doorway. It was the woman of the house, with the little man of the house right behind her.

"Bye, Jennifer! Thanks again," Rene said, waving.

"Bye, Jennifer!" CJ shouted.

It was hard for Jennifer to return the gesture, while her clitoris was pulsating, but she managed.

"Bye, y'all," she said before entering the safe confines of her car.

Everyone stepped inside, and Corey secured the door behind them. Rene's heart fluttered when he wrapped his arms around her and spoke softly in her ear.

"Why is your son still awake? Don't tell me I ate all of those oysters for nothing."

"Not a chance," Rene said with a chuckle. "I'll have him tucked-in in five minutes."

"Are y'all talking about me?" CJ wanted to know.

Corey kissed his wife on the lips rather than respond. He wasn't paying attention to his eager hands until the boy said, "*Ooh! Daddy touched your butt just like Jennifer!*"

Rene's body stiffened. Confusion marred her features as she backed away from her husband. To his credit, Corey looked as confused as she did. A sick chill enveloped Rene's body as she looked down at their child.

"What did you say?"

CJ's smile slipped when he saw his parents' reaction. "Uh..."

"He's talking crazy," Corey offered. "You know how kids are."

Rene's breaths came hot and heavy as she knelt to look the boy in his eyes. "What did you say? Did you see Daddy hug Ms. Jennifer?"

The child looked from his mother's concerned eyes to his father's guilty ones. CJ wasn't sure what he'd done wrong this time, but the mood in the living room certainly felt like trouble. He nodded hesitantly.

"I gave her a hug," Corey admitted. "It was just a quick, little side-to-side hug. There was nothing to it. I certainly didn't grab her butt."

"Did he?" Rene asked CJ, her eyes never leaving his. "Did your father touch Ms. Jennifer's behind?"

"No, I just told you I didn't," Corey interjected.

"Would you shut up and let the boy answer?" Rene snapped. She looked up at him, her eyes filled with venom.

But her orbs softened when she returned her attention to their son. "Did he?" she asked again. "Did you see Daddy touch Ms. Jennifer's behind?"

Corey's heart pumped dread through his veins while they waited for an answer. CJ looked from his mother to his father, and his eyes filled with tears. Rene waited, but the boy remained silent.

"This is silly," Corey told his wife. "You're stressing him out for nothing. Why would I touch that woman in my own home – *while you're here*? If I was gonna do something that stupid, I think I'd have enough sense to try to avoid getting caught. But I wouldn't do it in the first place," he quickly added. "CJ wasn't even in the room when I walked her out. I don't know what he *thinks* he saw, but I swear I didn't touch that woman – not like that."

Rene's eyes narrowed. She didn't appear to believe him, but one thing was for sure: This conversation was freaking out their son. Whatever had happened between Jennifer and Corey was not CJ's fault, and he didn't deserve to be put in the middle of it.

"Come on." She stood and took the boy's hand. "Let's get you to bed."

Corey sighed silently as they walked away, but he didn't allow relief to wash over him just yet. There was a chance Rene would interrogate CJ again when they got to his bedroom.

But she didn't stay in the boy's room long enough for that. Corey was still undressing when she entered the master bedroom and began to remove her own clothes. Corey was hoping to peel her jeans off himself and was a little chagrined to see her slip on an unflattering nightgown before climbing into bed. She rested with her back facing his side of the bed.

That was a clear indication there'd be no sex that night, but he dared to ask.

"So does this mean I ate all of those oysters for nothing?"

Rene sighed roughly and loudly. But other than that, she didn't respond.

Corey finished undressing and turned off the lights before getting into bed. He pleaded with her for a few minutes, reiterating his stance that CJ didn't know what he was talking about. Whatever the boy thought he saw was wrong.

But it didn't work. Rene feigned sleep, and after a while, Corey rolled to his side and gave in to Mr. Sandman.

CHAPTER THREE

Sunday morning's sun leaked through slats in the blinds and sprayed the bedroom with rays bright enough to wake a hibernating bear. Even with his back facing the window, Corey couldn't ignore the slow rising fireball's beam.

"Baby, close the blinds," Corey mumbled.

When Rene didn't respond he turned over—wincing like he'd been stabbed—and used his forearm to shield his eyes.

Rene was gone. In fact, she hadn't been in the bed since five o'clock that morning.

Corey rolled back on his side and squinted to see the clock on his nightstand. "Seven-fifty," he mumbled. "Rene never gets up this early in the morning on Sunday."

Corey remained on his side with his back to the window until his vision cleared. He was determined to stay there a little longer, but the scent of bacon and fresh coffee joined forces and disrupted his plans. The blended aromas snaked out of the kitchen and into the bedroom—just as Rene intended.

Rene sat at the kitchen table staring at the coffee in her mug. She used a spoon to stir the dark roast blend in a clockwise motion while she waited for it to cool. Rene loved the serenity that accompanied Sunday mornings. Going to church to watch a pastor gyrate and shout while spouting a recycled sermon wasn't her thing. But, she made it a point to pray and meditate while no one was stirring.

Corey always seemed bothered by Rene's Sunday morning ritual. In fact, the quieter she became the more his boyish ways surfaced. He'd often try to talk to her during her respite, and would get agitated when she ignored him.

'Oh, I forgot...I married a woman of few words on Sunday', he'd say.

Rene's eyes rolled behind her closed lids every time she heard his sarcasm. Her annoyance was heightened because after ten years of marriage she felt he still didn't *know* her.

'Still waters run deep', was Rene's standard reply to Corey's uninformed comment. It was her subtle way of reminding him to not mistake her decision to *say* little as an inability to *think* a lot.

The sound of Corey's shoulder brushing against the wall could be heard before he staggered into the kitchen. He let out a loud yawn as he cleared the hallway, stuck his index finger into his ear, and wiggled it—a practice he swore helped him with his sinuses.

Rene often jumped at the opportunity to ridicule his annoying habit, but she was in no mood for small talk or playful banter on this Sunday morning. As the coffee mug made it to her pursed lips all she could think about was CJ's innocent, but explosive, comment about his father.

"How long you been up, bae?"

"Since five," Rene replied in that bland, *you're on my shit list so don't try to make small talk,* tone that all women seem to be born with.

41

"That bacon smells good," Corey said and kissed her on the forehead. "You got some more?"

Rene nodded toward the far counter. "I put some on that plate for you."

Corey opened a cabinet and scanned until he spotted the Dallas Cowboys coffee cup Rene gave him as a Father's Day gift. He filled the cup with coffee and took a swig.

"Damn, that's strong."

"Just like you like it," Rene said.

Corey nodded and grabbed the plate of pork. "Those oysters were good last night, but they didn't stick to my ribs. I feel like I haven't eaten in days." He shoved a piece of bacon in his mouth and spoke while chewing. "I've gotta get something on my stomach before I meet Wayne for a round of golf."

"What's your tee time?"

"Ten."

"You'd better hurry," Rene said and sipped her coffee without looking at him.

The tension in the room was thick enough to cut with a knife. Corey knew he was in the doghouse even though Rene hadn't announced it. Rene wasn't the screaming type. Her anger simmered like a pot of gumbo. But Corey was also aware that Rene knew his tendencies. He was a talker. Silence was the equivalent of a taped confession of guilt.

"What'cha got goin' on today?" Corey asked in a feeble attempt to thaw Rene's frosty exterior.

"Nothing." Rene put her cup down. "I intend to sit here and think."

"About what?" Corey asked, eyeballing his bacon. It took a few seconds for him to realize he'd opened *Pandora's*

Box with his response, but by the time he looked at his wife it was too late.

Corey's question slid out of his mouth without permission. In his mind he could see the words "about" and "what" hurling through the air; tumbling like asteroids floating in space. He desperately wanted to drop his coffee cup, push the plate of bacon to the side, and lunge across the kitchen table with his arms and fingers extended hoping to snag the "t's" at the end of each word. But sleep hadn't completely released the grip it had on his reflexes. Before he could move, Rene looked up from her coffee mug and locked onto his crusty eyes.

Aww shit, Corey thought. He shoved more bacon into his mouth before another foolish question could escape.

Yeah, mother-fucka. I got your ass right where I want you, Rene thought before mounting her attack. "I guess I'll spend a little more time thinking about CJ's comment when we got home last night. You know...the one where he said he saw his father touching the babysitter's ass."

Corey's eyes widened. He rubbed the back of his neck and stuffed another strip of bacon inside of his already crowded mouth. Too much pork and not enough chewing led to a choking bout that forced him to gulp the hot coffee until the tide washed the bacon down. When he looked at Rene he could tell he might have been better off letting asphyxiation be a diversionary tactic.

"Bae, I told you last night," Corey paused to wipe the tears that formed in his eyes after his near death experience, "Lil Man doesn't know what he's talkin' 'bout."

"You know, I'm glad you said that," Rene replied and wagged her finger at him.

"Said what?"

"You called CJ, *Lil Man*. That reminded me of something that crossed my mind last night."

Corey looked more nervous than a KKK member asked to speak at a Black Panther rally. He used his hand to wipe away the coffee that splattered on his cheek and chin. "I always call him, Lil Man."

"Umm hmm," Rene grunted and stood up. She folded her arms and paced in a tight circle behind her chair for a few seconds before speaking. "When was the last time you've seen Jennifer?"

Corey shrugged. "I don't know...months."

Rene gazed at him for a second and paced some more. "When was the last time Jennifer babysat CJ?"

Corey shrugged again. "I don't know," he said and stared aimlessly at the refrigerator, "six months."

"Try more than a year," Rene said, still pacing with her arms folded while she stared down at her feet.

"Okay...a year. What's your point?"

Rene leaned against the counter. "Since we both agree that it's been a little over a year since Jennifer saw our child, how is it she knew his nickname?"

Corey shrugged so hard his shoulders grazed his earlobes. "I don't know. She must have heard me say it yesterday."

"Impossible," Rene said, her head shaking like a child refusing to eat broccoli. "Ya see, when Jennifer arrived you were in the shower. The first thing she did was speak to CJ."

"And?"

Rene moved away from the counter, placed her hands on the table—palms down—and leaned forward like she was in the starting blocks at a track meet.

"Jennifer referred to my baby as, Lil Man."

44

Corey took another gulp of his coffee. If he had proof—or even heard rumors—that clicking his heels three times could make him vanish, he would have tried it.

"Bae, I don't know," Corey replied and carried the plate and coffee cup over to the sink. "You're asking me a question I don't have an answer to. Now, I've gotta get dressed and head to the golf course."

Rene watched him vanish around the corner. She sat down and grabbed her mug. Her coffee was cold, but she was too angry to care.

"You can run from this conversation, but I'm not through!" she said. "You have until the end of your golf round to come clean or else I'm inviting Jennifer over here today so the three of us can have a little chat!"

"Are you finished?" Corey shouted from down the hall.

Rene sipped her coffee and replied, "For now."

Corey arrived at Brookhaven Country Club fifteen minutes before Wayne did. They were both average golfers at best, but the business connections they made more than offset the frustration and humiliation that accompanied the sport.

In fact, while playing in a foursome one year earlier, Corey met Bronson O'Neill, President of O'Neill Properties. Bronson's company specialized in managing shopping malls. Much to Corey's delight, Bronson's golfing skills were on par with his own. As a result, they were able to empathize with each other's struggles and form a rapport.

Laughs on the course led to a round of drinks. That round of drinks became the launch pad for several rounds of negotiations which landed Corey the shopping mall contract he and his wife went out to celebrate the night before.

Corey leaned against his car with his arms crossed until he couldn't take it any longer. He pulled out his phone and was about to dial Wayne's number when he saw his best friend's Tesla swerve into the parking area.

"You ready for this ass whipping?" Wayne shouted from the car window as he pulled into the space next to Corey. He hopped out the car like a superhero who'd guzzled too many energy drinks.

"Calm your ass down," Corey said, his eyes darting around the parking lot to see if there were members within earshot. "You act like you just snorted a line."

"I'm hyped, dog!" Wayne retrieved his golf bag from the back seat of his car. "I got my balls licked and my nipples pinched last night, and now I'm ready to beat yo' yella ass like you stole somethin'." Wayne paused long enough to give Corey some dap. "I suggest you call one of your security officers and tell 'em to come over and protect you from this beat down I'm about to issue."

Corey waved dismissively. "Man, shut up and lets go play...ole fake ass Tiger Woods."

The two friends talked about everything from politics to sports for the first three holes of golf, but the conversation got serious as they prepared to tackle the fourth hole.

"What's wrong, bruh?" Wayne asked.

"I'm cool," Corey mumbled.

Wayne pulled his driver out of his bag and waved it at Corey. "Nigga, don't make me hit you with this driver. I've known you since college. Remember, I was the first person you confided in when you lost your virginity. I know all of your secrets so don't get shy now." Wayne approached the tee, coiled his body, and struck the ball like a pro. "Yeah, boy!" he shouted and then posed in his stance. "I'm ready to go pro."

"In your dreams," Corey said.

Corey used his elbow to nudge Wayne out of the way and then placed his tee in the ground. After a few practice swings he approached the ball and swung. The ball traveled one hundred yards—into the tree line.

"I may be dreaming about becoming a pro golfer," Wayne said as he boarded their golf cart, "but I ain't dreaming when I say something is wrong with you." He started the golf cart once Corey climbed aboard. "I'll drive. You talk."

Corey pulled a Cuban cigar from his golf bag. He bit the tip off and spat it out. After taking a moment to discard a few strands of tobacco that hung from the tip like dreadlocks, he lit the end of the cigar—turning it slowly to ensure an even burn—and puffed until it had an ashy afro.

"Ole fake ass Suge Knight," Wayne said. "Nigga, tell me what's goin' on. We ain't got all day."

"It's Rene."

"What about her?"

"She heard something about me."

"One of your freaks called her?"

"No."

"They reached out to her on Facebook, huh?" Wayne said and shook his head. "Man, I told you to discourage her from getting on Facebook. That shit is kryptonite to a playa. You can't even get away with fucking dumb bitches no more. Even they're smart enough to find a way to contact your woman on Facebook."

"No one contacted Rene on Facebook. The snitch was my son."

Wayne frowned like he got a whiff of a fart. "CJ?"

"Yep, my baby boy snitched on me," Corey replied while puffing his cigar; his words mingled with the smoke and swirled in the space between he and Wayne.

Wayne pulled the golf cart to the side of the path and turned it off. "What happened?"

"Did I ever tell you about the little fine babysitter we have named Jennifer?"

Wayne thought for a moment. "Yeah, you showed me a picture of her. Little sexy redbone, right?"

"That's the one," Corey confirmed. "Well, I've been fucking her for a few months."

Wayne put his forehead on the steering wheel. "Bruh, please tell me you didn't fuck that chick in your house and CJ caught you."

"He didn't catch me fucking her, but he did catch me rubbing her ass."

"And he told Rene?"

Corey nodded.

Wayne shook his head in disgust. "Ya see, I told you to put CJ's little ass in a nursery in South Dallas. If he was around more black kids he'd know snitches get stitches." Wayne looked at Corey and shook his head pitifully. "What did Rene say?"

"She's pissed," Corey said, and contorted his mouth to make smoke rings.

"You denied that shit right?"

"C'mon, dog," Corey said and looked at Wayne as if he was appalled by the question, "you know I wrote the Playa Manual. Chapter five, paragraph six—"

"Deny until you die," Wayne blurted out.

"You damn right," Corey said and gave Wayne some dap. "But with my track record, she ain't gon' believe me."

Wayne started the golf cart. "Man, don't worry about that shit. She didn't catch you fuckin' her so you're good."

"I wish it was that simple. She told me before I left the house this morning that if I don't come clean when I get back she's going to call Jennifer and tell her to come over so the three of us can have a *chat*."

"Damn," Wayne said. He rubbed his chin and thought for a moment. Suddenly, his eyes widened and he snapped his fingers. "Do some of the security guards at your company have weapons?"

"About half of them do. Why?"

"You need to put a hit out on Jennifer. Because if Rene contacts her," Wayne looked over his shoulder to make sure no other golf carts were coming before he merged back onto the path, "your ass is through."

"Dog, I know you're bullshitting, but you're right. After I got busted gettin' head from that flight attendant two years ago, Rene threatened to leave me and go back to California with my son."

"First of all, you got busted because you got a blow job at a park three blocks away from your house. You knew Rene drove past that park every day. That was just stupid." Wayne paused. His eyebrows arched and he rubbed his chin as a thought crossed his mind. "Actually, the more I think about it, it could've been worse."

"What's worse than her catchin' me get a blow job?"

"Her catchin' you *giving* a blow job," Wayne replied.

"True dat," Corey said and chuckled. "Honestly, it doesn't matter when, where, or how I got busted, what matters is she threatened to divorce me and take my child out of the state if I got busted *peeking* at another woman."

"You're in deep shit, playa," Wayne said.

"YesssIAmmmm," Corey replied, connecting the words in exasperation.

Wayne stopped the cart when they were within a few feet of where his golf ball landed.

"I suggest you try to plea bargain."

"What do you mean?"

"I mean, cop to having a weak moment and squeezing the girl's ass. That's the lesser crime—take the charge. Rene will be pissed and will ban her from coming around, but at least she won't try to dig deeper into the situation and possibly find out you've been bangin' the chick for months."

"True," Corey said.

"She's going to need you to acknowledge her value so agree to give her anything she wants."

"*Anything*?"

Wayne looked at Corey. "Yeah, ma'fucka...*anything!*"

"I don't know 'bout that," Corey said. "If I start showering her with gifts because I squeezed a chick's ass, that's going to set a dangerous precedent."

"Suit yourself," Wayne replied. He paused to study the distance to the putting green and then approached his golf ball. "Seems to me, giving her whatever she wants beats the hell out of losing the ability to see your son everyday..." Wayne swung and hit the ball. After staring at the ball's flight he looked at Corey, "...and losing half of your company, investments, and everything you own in a divorce settlement."

Rene fought back tears while preparing CJ's breakfast. She knew in her heart that Corey was guilty of doing what CJ accused him of. She'd put up with ten years of infidelity. Ten years of weak alibis. Ten years of giving him *second* chances. Groping wasn't as bad as catching him getting a blow job from a flight attendant or learning he'd had sex with Brazilian floozies while on one of his *bro trips*. But, when a woman's at her wits end, a comparitively innocent infraction like groping someone is enough to qualify as a dealbreaker.

"CJ, come eat your food!"

"Mama, I wanna watch, *Cars*."

"You can watch that movie later. For now, I want you to come sit at the table and eat your breakfast."

"But, mama, I wanna watch the movie."

Rene smacked the counter. "Corey Junior, come sit at this table right now!"

"I want my daddy," CJ muttered as he dragged his feet while walking to the table.

"You and every other woman around," Rene said and placed a plate covered with eggs on the table. She put two strips of bacon on top of the eggs and slid a glass of orange juice next to the plate. "Sit down and eat. And you're not watching that movie until you finish."

Rene sat down. She rested her elbows on top of the table and buried her face in the palms of her hands. Her hands hid her tears, but couldn't mute her sniffling.

"What's wrong, mama?"

"Nothing, baby," Rene used the heels of her hands to dab her eyes. "Mama's eyes hurt. Eat your food while I make a phone call."

Rene needed someone to talk to. Her parents, who were now deceased, only had one child. Not having to share toys, clothes, and gifts with a sibling made Rene somewhat privileged growing up, but she'd been robbed of the support a sibling can provide. As a result, she'd spent a lifetime seeking the counsel of friends during her times of need.

"Who are you callin', mama?"

"Aunt Jackie," Rene said and walked away from the table. "Eat your food and be quiet while I talk to her."

Jacquelyn Flemming was a two time divorcee with attitude galore and more opinions than a radio talk show host. Rene met Jackie during her undergrad years at Stanford University when they were both newbies on the volleyball team. Jackie was a rebel in every sense of the word. She was Rene's alter ego—the person that often said and did the things Rene wished she had the courage to do. Jackie wasn't always right, but she was always brutally honest. The type of unfiltered friend every person needs.

"He did what!" Jackie shouted.

"You heard me," Rene said.

"In front of CJ?"

"Yes."

"Oh, hell to the no! Rene, I know you ain't gon' stand for that shit. Not after what he did the last time. You promised me that if you caught him even looking at another woman too long you were going to dump his big head ass."

"I know what I said, Jackie."

"Well, if you know what you said the last time, I've got one question for you."

"What?"

"Bitch...what you gon' do?"

"Trust me, I got a plan," Rene said confidently.

"Well, I hope it includes getting you some outside dick because you've got a *cheat receipt*."

"A what?"

"A *cheat receipt*," Jackie repeated. "I was driving through Mississippi last month on my way to Jackson to attend a conference. All they play on the radio in that area is the Blues. Girl, I heard a song that had me laughing out loud. It was called, *Cheat Receipt*. The song was about a woman who caught her man cheating and as a result, she had a free pass to do the same thing his ass was out there doing."

"Yeah, but the person that made that song doesn't stand to lose everything I can lose if I get caught cheating. Corey would probably sic one of those high powered lawyers he's met at that country club on me. You gon' take care of me and my baby if I get caught cashing in my *cheat receipt*?"

"Girl, I can barely take care of myself," Jackie said.

"That's my point. I've got to be smart."

"Smart my ass," Jackie said. "You should get his ass back by fuckin' one of his friends. And I've got the perfect one in mind."

"Who?"

"Heifer you know who," Jackie fired back. "You forget that I've been ridin' with you damn near twenty years. I was with you when you met Corey's cheating ass at our volleyball tournament in Atlanta."

"I know you were."

"Then you should also know that I remember how it all went down. Corey was the one flirting with you, but yo'sneaky ass was checking out Wayne."

"Damn, girl," Rene blurted out, "do you remember everything?"

"Yep. I remember how you were drooling over Wayne, but he was too busy flirting with those girls on the other team. You gave Corey some *play* to take your mind off of his friend. The rest is history."

"Be quiet."

"I'll be quiet, but take my advice, if you really wanna stick it to your unfaithful ass husband you're going to have to hit him where it hurts. If you wanna stop him from going around screwing flight attendants and flirting with babysitters in your house—in front of your child—ride his best friend's dick. Let him see how it feels to be disrespected."

"Trust me, I'm going to get him back," Rene said. "I've got leverage on his ass," she said pausing to use a napkin to dab her runny nose, "and I intend to use it."

CHAPTER FOUR

Corey called his side chick on the way home from his golf outing.

"Hello?"

"Hey, has my wife called you?"

After a pause, Jennifer said, "What?"

"I think you heard what I said."

"You mean today? You know I talked to her yesterday."

He sighed gruffly. "Yes, I mean today."

"Why you getting an attitude?"

"'Cause it's some shit going down, and I just need you to answer the fucking question."

"No, she hasn't called me. Are you gonna tell me what's wrong?"

Corey told her what happened last night.

"Shit," Jennifer breathed. "I knew you shouldn't have been touching me like that in your house."

"Well, it's not like you told me to stop. Even if you did, this ain't a good time for an *I told you so*."

"Okay. Fine. What are you gonna do? *Dammit*. Rene knows my parents. I don't want her telling them about this."

"I only got two choices," Corey said. "I can either tell her I grabbed your ass, cop to the lesser charge—"

"*Lesser charge?*"

"Yeah. That's better than telling her I been fucking you."

"Yeah. Okay."

"Or I can deny everything and wait for her to call you."

"What's she gonna do if you admit to touching me?"

"I don't know." Corey sighed. He was traveling the speed limit on the interstate, but he felt like he was speeding. He was getting too close to his confrontation with his wife way too quickly. "She might leave me."

"Then don't tell her," Jennifer suggested.

"You think I should deny everything?"

"Yes. Like you said, she might leave you either way, so why risk it?"

"She's gonna call you as soon as I talk to her."

"It's cool. I'll deny everything too. I'll tell her you just gave me a side-to-side hug, like you already told her. If we both say the same thing, she'll have to believe us over CJ."

A sweet flood of relief washed over Corey. He knew Jennifer was a good side-piece, but he didn't think she was this good. "Are you sure? She's gonna grill the shit outta your ass. You think you can stand up to her?"

"Yeah. Why not? What's she gonna do, jump through the phone and strangle me?"

Corey chuckled nervously. "No, she can't do that."

"Then stop sweating it."

"You do understand this is my whole life we're talking about, don't you? This is something I definitely need to be sweating."

"Baby, you gotta trust me. I know what this means to you, and I'm not gonna be the one to fuck up your life. Plus, I don't want Rene calling my parents with this bullshit, calling me a home wrecker."

"Okay," Corey said, his resolve now restored. "So we'll both deny it to the bitter end, and she'll have to let it go."

"Sounds like a plan," Jennifer said.

Despite her assurances, tendrils of doubt tried to wrap Corey up like an octopus, but he fought it off. This was the plan, and it was a good one. It would work, because it had to.

"Okay. I'll talk to you later."

"Alright, baby."

"Expect her to call you in about thirty minutes."

"Okay."

"Can you text me after you talk to her, to let me know what she said?"

"Yeah. I will."

"Oh, one more thing: She's gonna ask why you call our son 'Lil Man.' She thinks you got the nickname from me."

"I did get that from you."

"But you can't tell her that."

"Everybody calls little boys that," Jennifer said. "I don't think that nickname is very unique."

"You're gonna tell her you came up with it on your own?"

"Yeah, if she asks."

"Okay." Corey sighed again. He couldn't think of anything else to prepare her for. "Alright. Talk to you later," he said and disconnected.

When he got home, Corey found his wife of ten years waiting for him in the kitchen. His son did not rush to greet him, as was CJ's custom. Rene watched him like a hawk as he stepped closer. She did not rise from her seat at the kitchen table. The tension in the room was so thick, Corey felt like he was wading through an invisible pool.

"Where's CJ?" he asked.

Rene's eyes never left his. Hers were hard and unreadable. His were anxious and guarded.

"He's having lunch with his grandma."

Rene's parents had passed away, so Corey knew she was referring to his mother. He also knew Rene had gotten their son out of the way for what she thought would be a monumental argument.

Corey maintained eye contact as he took a seat across from her. He reminded himself that without a confession from Jennifer, Rene's theory about what may or may not have happened last night meant nothing. He took a deep breath and blew it out slowly. His palms were sweating, but he was pretty sure there was no perspiration on his forehead. He dared not reach up to check.

"Listen," he said, "I know you wanna argue about what CJ said, but I don't. What I told you last night is the same thing I'm gonna tell you now: I did not touch Jennifer like that. I would not do anything that stupid in my own home, with you just a few feet away. I know I've cheated in the past, and you have to keep your guard up. That's my fault. I made you the way you are. You have a right to be suspicious, and you have a right to believe what CJ told you. But I didn't do it."

Rene watched him for a while before speaking. Corey knew she was using her motherly lie-detector to read every nuance of his features. He tried to maintain a neutral expression, but it was impossible to know if whatever subtle twitch she was looking for was present. He didn't bite his lip or look away from her, of that much he was sure.

Rene began to shake her head slowly. Corey's heart knocked like a bass drum while he waited for her to respond. He swallowed roughly, knowing that might be one of the telltale signs of deception she was looking for, but he couldn't help it.

"I just, I find it hard to believe CJ would make up something like that," she said. "Are you sure your hand didn't brush her ass at all, maybe as you were backing away?"

Corey's eyes widened slightly. He couldn't believe what he was hearing. Did she just give him an out? If so, he was ready to jump on it!

"Uh, well, um, I guess something like that might have happened," he conceded. "I wasn't paying attention to every little move I made. It was just a quick hug, as far as I know. But, yeah. Maybe my hand did brush her when we backed away."

Rene's nostrils flared as she took in a deep breath. She continued to stare at him so intently, Corey felt like she could see every bit of him, all the way to his soul. "Do you swear to me that you didn't grab her ass?"

"I didn't, baby."

"Do you *swear*?"

"I swear. I swear to you, babe."

She watched him for a while longer and then nodded. "Okay," she finally said.

Corey's eyes registered confusion. "Okay?"

She nodded. "Yeah. Okay."

His head tilted slowly to the side. "Okay, you believe me?"

She nodded. "Yes. I have no reason not to – do I?"

"No. No, you don't," he said quickly. "I'm telling you the truth."

"Okay," she said again. "Then I believe you."

While this was what Corey wanted to happen, he had a hard time accepting it. It seemed too good to be true. But he was never one to look a gift horse in the mouth. "Alright, soooo... are we done talking about this?"

Rene continued to nod. "I'm done. I'm sorry I accused you of something you didn't do. Do you want me to make you something for lunch?"

Corey's look of confusion deepened. Not only was she letting him off the hook, but she was the one apologizing? This was an incredible turn of events! "Uh, sure," he said. "Thanks."

He rose from his seat and headed for the back door. "I'm, uh, I'm gonna go water the garden."

"Okay," Rene said. She stood as well. "Lunch will be ready in about twenty minutes."

Corey looked back at her before stepping through the back door. Rene had her back to him as she rummaged through the fridge. Corey shook his head and continued on his way.

Five minutes later he was still spraying water on a beautiful garden that had done very well that season. Their tomato plants were decorated with swollen fruit that were almost ready for picking. Even their strawberries had thrived this year. Plucking the treat straight from the source and popping it into his mouth after a quick rinse was one of Corey's joys. But he didn't have the appetite for such things today.

He held the spray nozzle of the hose in one hand and a cigarette in the other. He had quit smoking, other than the occasional cigar, years ago. But today he picked up a pack of his old favorites on the way home from the golf course. The coffin nails, aka Newports, tasted as great as they always had. They were so good, in fact, Corey wondered why he ever let Rene talk him into giving them up.

He looked back to make sure he was still alone in the backyard before tossing the butt of his cigarette into the garden. He sprayed it with the hose to make sure it was extinguished before pushing a little dirt over it with his foot. The wet soil left a muddy stain on his golf shoe. Corey cursed himself and his wife as he turned and walked away from the garden.

Rather than head back inside, he took a seat on one of the patio chairs. The patio was covered, so there was no glare on his cellphone display. He hadn't missed any texts from Jennifer. He grunted as he dug the pack of cigarettes from his pocket. He lit up another one and tried to relax as he waited. Ten minutes later he was on his third cigarette, and *finally* his cellphone buzzed in his hand. He tossed his cigarette into the lawn as he read Jennifer's message:

She called me.

No surprise there. Corey quickly typed, What she say?

She asked if you touched my butt. I told her no.

A slight sneer distorted the corner of Corey's mouth. He knew Rene didn't believe him. But why not just say it when they were talking?

He typed, Was that it?

She replied, Pretty much.

He typed, I don't wanna hear pretty much. Tell me everything.

Want me to call you?

Bitch, hell naw! Corey thought, his face scrunched up. He typed, Hell no!

She replied, Too much to type.

Hoe, you better get those fingers working! Corey thought. He calmed himself and typed, Please.

After thirty seconds, he got another message: She asked if you touched me at all. I said you hugged me, but you didn't do anything inappropriate. She asked why I called CJ Lil Man. I told her I don't know. It's just something I call little boys. She said okay, and that was it.

Corey didn't think that was too much to type at all.

Was that all she said? She believed you?

Yes. She said she was sorry for bothering me and hung up.

Wow. Corey felt like the god of infidelity had truly blessed him. He hadn't felt this relieved since his mother's breast cancer scare.

Okay, ttyl, he told Jennifer.

He was still grinning at his phone when Rene stepped outside. She looked from his dopey expression to the phone in his hand and then to the cigarette butts in the yard.

"You smoking again?" she asked him.

"Uh, no, not really," Corey said reflexively.

Rene's eyes narrowed.

Corey realized this particular lie was pointless. The evidence was right before their eyes. Plus, he had been lying to his wife all morning. After the bullet he just dodged, the least he could do was be honest about smoking.

"I've been under a lot of stress," he explained. "I thought you weren't gonna believe me, about what happened with Jennifer. I honestly thought my life was ruined. So, yeah. I bought a pack of squares. I'm sorry."

She surprised him by saying, "It's okay. Are you ready to eat lunch?"

Corey began to suspect that whatever she was feeding him might be poisoned, but he forced a smile and nodded. "Yeah. I guess I am kinda hungry."

Over the next couple of weeks, Corey's apprehension gradually ebbed as he and his wife settled back into their normal groove. For the first couple of days, he slept with one eye open, thinking Rene hadn't really accepted his or Jennifer's version of events. But each day Corey woke up and found his dick still attached to his body, rather than sitting on the pillow next to him, he realized he actually had gotten away with cheating yet again.

That should've been enough to make him keep his hands to himself and save his sweet loving for the woman he promised to have and to hold, in sickness and health, till death did them part. But as beautiful as Rene was, she wasn't enough to stop Corey's wayward dick from wanting more. He called his best friend from work one afternoon, hoping Wayne could talk him out of doing something foolish.

"What's up?"

"I'm getting the itch," Corey confided. "I think I need counseling, man. I'm fucked up in the head."

After a laugh, Wayne said, "I know you ain't talking about cheating again."

"I am," Corey countered. "I'm sick, man. I need help, right?"

"I don't know about all that. But you do need to take a step back and reevaluate your life. Didn't you almost get busted two weeks ago?"

"Yeah. I still don't know how I talked my way out of that one."

"You and Rene are in a good place now?"

"Yeah. Everything's back to normal. But that only means *I'm* back to normal. And normal for me is, you know, seeking excitement whenever I can."

"You know if she catches you again it's over."

"Yeah," Corey grumbled, "I know." He leaned forward with his forearms on his desk.

"She might cut your dick off."

"Man, don't say that. I been sleeping with a hand in my boxers for a week. I know Rene's watching everything I do."

"If you know all that, why don't you just chill? It ain't like your wife ain't got it going on. Matter of fact, there's a million men in this city alone who'd throw their wife in the gutter to get with Rene."

"Why don't *you* ever chill?" Corey countered. "You have a different woman on your arm every time I see you."

"Bruh, I'm not married. I'm allowed to do that. If you wanna live my lifestyle, get a divorce."

"I can't," Corey said with a sigh. "I don't wanna break up my family. Plus, the way our prenup is set up, I'd be ruined if I leave her for no reason."

"Then do the same thing every married man does when he wants some *new-new*," Wayne suggested.

"What's that?"

"Go to PornHub, get some lotion, and handle your business. Just don't tell me about it."

Corey smacked his lips. "Nigga please. The ones who do that can't get nothing better. But I can."

"Don't do it," Wayne said seriously. "You called me for advice, and that's the advice I'm giving you. Don't cheat on Rene."

After a few beats, Corey told him, "Thanks. That's what I needed to hear, man."

"Alright. You good?"

"Yeah. I'ma finish up a few things here and take off."

"Alright. I'll holler at you."

Corey disconnected and leaned back in his executive chair. He propped his feet on his desk and stared down at his cellphone. He knew he was up to no good as he scrolled through his contacts, because the hairs stood on his arms and neck. His breaths came short and quick. He felt like a crackhead staring at a perfectly good rock, but for some reason, he wasn't allowed to smoke it.

By the time he got to the P's in his contact list, there was no doubt about what he was going to do. He had Jennifer's number saved as *PT*. Only he knew that stood for *"Pretty Toes."* His pulse raced as he dialed her number. She answered after a couple of rings.

"Didn't expect to hear from you again."

"Oh yeah?" Corey said, trying to sound like he wasn't close to hyperventilating. "And why is that?"

"You know why. Is your wife off your back already?"

"Everything's good on my end."

"If everything's good, why you wanna be bad?"

Jennifer didn't sound like she was trying to be sexy, but her voice sent a jolt from Corey's chest, straight down to his manhood. He brought a hand to his lap and stroked himself through his pants while they talked.

"I don't know how to be good," he said honestly. "I just know how to be me."

She giggled. "And who are you?"

"I'm the man who said I was gonna stuff something in your mouth for talking shit the last time I saw you. If you scared, tell me now. If you not, get in your car, and come to my office. I'm only gonna be here for another hour."

An eternity passed while he waited for her to respond. Corey got so hard in the interim, he wondered if he should rub one out before she got there – if she decided to come.

She finally said, "I can't be there in an hour. I gotta take a shower first."

Corey's heart started to kick again, this time with the sweet beat of anticipation. He told her, "If you keep me waiting, those toes better be clean as a whistle."

"They will be," she promised. "See you soon."

Corey disconnected and considered backing out. He told the little angel on his shoulder to go to hell and called his wife.

Rene's phone rang three times. Each time, the tone sounded like *DOOOOON'TDOIT, DOOOOON'TDOIT, DOOOOON'TDOIT.*

"Hey, baby," she answered.

"Hey, um, I'ma be late tonight," he told her.

She said, "Okay. I can reheat your dinner when you get here."

Corey was shocked that she didn't question him or hesitate at all. That made him feel guiltier than the adultery he was about to commit.

"Thanks, baby," he told her. "You're the best."

An hour and a half later, Corey had Jennifer on her knees next to his desk. She wore a short skirt with a flirty halter top that exposed plenty of succulent flesh about the shoulders and stomach. She wasn't talking noise at the moment, but a promise is a promise. Corey stood over her with his hands on his hips.

He could've done the honors himself, but he told her, "Unbuckle my belt." He watched as she did so.

"You don't have to be so mean," she said. Her eyes were flirty. Her lips glistened with a thin coat of fuchsia colored lipstick. Overall she oozed sexuality.

"You should've thought of that when you were talking noise the other day."

"What did I even say?" she asked as she unfastened his belt. The bulge of his erection swelled beneath his slacks.

"You know what you said." Corey's breaths were slow and hot. His stomach tightened when she started unbuttoning his pants.

"You don't even remember, do you?" she said with a chuckle. "You're just being mean for the sake of being mean."

She was right about that, on both parts. But Corey wasn't going to let a little thing like logic spoil his role-playing.

"That shit you're saying right now is what I'm talking about," he told her.

He reached and grabbed a handful of her luscious locks, which was a big no-no for some sisters. But Jennifer didn't complain about him damaging her weave.

She just said, "*Ow,*" and winced a little.

"Unzip my pants," he demanded, squeezing her hair tighter.

"*I am,*" she said. "What do you think I'm–"

He jerked her head to the side, to let her know he meant business. "You doing a lot of talking, and not enough unzipping," he growled.

She got his zipper down. His manhood poked his boxers so hard it looked uncomfortable, so she pulled them down too. The sight of his hard piece pointing at her nose made her eyes dilate.

"Alright," she said, "Can you let go of my *haai –* *mmph!*"

Corey made good on his promise to shut her up. Jennifer's eyes widened, but she wasn't completely shocked by the move. If she was, her teeth would've been an effective barrier. But she opened wide, and he slid in with no discomfort. Surprise was part of the game, however, so she looked up at him indignantly as he pushed deeper into her mouth.

She mumbled something unintelligible. Corey pumped his hips a few times, enough to cause a bit of pre-cum to squirt on her tongue, before he pulled out and said, "What?"

"Could you let go of my hair?" she asked again.

He loosened his grip but didn't stop palming the back of her head as he slid in again. *Good Gawd* the woman had skills. Her cheeks went concave as she sucked him in deeper. Her tongue provided constant titillation to his shaft and the sensitive spot under the head.

She started to work her neck, and Corey's eyes rolled to the back of his head. Everything she was doing felt wonderful, but he didn't want her to participate in that manner. He gripped her hair again, this time with both hands, and held her head still.

"Don't move," he commanded.

Jennifer's nostrils flared as she stared up at him. She really looked pissed now. Corey sneered back at her and started to pump his hips again. Jennifer continued to work her lips and tongue as he fucked her face.

Oh my gawd! Corey nearly lost it that quickly. He wondered how someone so young could be so skilled. A pang of jealousy hit him as he considered all of the men she'd serviced in her lifetime. It was ridiculous for him to care, but the jealousy fueled his make-believe anger, so he ran with it.

He pulled out and told her, "Stand up."

When she didn't comply quickly enough, he pulled her up by the hair.

"*I said get up.*"

Jennifer was a willing participant, but even role-playing had its limits. Her eyes flashed real anger when she made it to her feet.

"Boy, you better—"

"Shut up!"

Corey spun her around and shoved her forward, bending her over his desk. He yanked her skirt up and her panties down in two quick motions. With her big, beautiful ass in his face, he forgot about her pretty toes and nearly forgot about a condom, but he hadn't made it this far in his whoring by being careless.

He told her, "Don't move," as he made his way to the front of his desk.

With his pants and boxers around his ankles, he knew his duck walk was comical. He wasn't surprised to see Jennifer smirking at him when he yanked the bottom drawer open and grabbed a box of condoms.

"I'ma give you something to laugh at," he told her.

He liberated a condom from its wrapper and waddled back into position. *Jesus.* Jennifer had a gorgeous ass! He pulled her skirt and panties all the way off and spread her legs. He could see that despite her protests, his antics were a turn-on. Her lips glistened with her essence.

He took a few moments to admire the glories of her anatomy before slamming in hard. She grunted in pleasure and pain. Her hands slid across the desk, reaching for something to grab hold of, but there were only papers and file folders. Corey was only mildly perturbed when she sent these items fluttering to the floor.

"Yeah. I got your ass now," he muttered.

To his surprise, Jennifer looked back at him and said, "Nigga, you ain't doing shit."

Corey's jaw dropped. "Oh yeah?"

He increased the power and depths of his thrusts until her squeals drowned out the sound of his thighs slapping her ass. He knew the housekeepers would hear them for sure, but what good is being a CEO if you can't do whatever the hell you want in your own office?

Even still, he told Jennifer, "*Shhh*. You know there's a few people still in the building."

"I'm try – I'm trying to be quiet," she told him. "It's too good. *Your dick's too good*!"

Corey felt the same way about her wet center. Her kitty was perfect for him. She was dripping wet, and her walls squeezed him just right. He could've cum at that moment, but he wanted to take his time with her. He wanted to flip her over and suck her toes and stare down at her as he penetrated again. He wanted to watch her expression when *she* came, with her toes in his mouth. Only then would he tend to his own needs.

Corey marveled at his good fortunes as he stroked his mistress long and hard. He had his own company, millions of dollars in assets, and a woman half his age sprawled out on his desk.

Life didn't get any better than this.

CHAPTER FIVE

Getting busted and being asked by his wife or girlfriend to have sex after he's just *blown his load* while having sex with his *sidepiece*, are the two things that strike the most fear in an unfaithful man.

Corey was well aware of those two scenarios, but spent little time pondering them on his way home. After all, he'd avoided getting busted a few weeks earlier when Rene bought his story. And because an air of tension blanketed their abode like the fog hovering over San Francisco Bay, the odds of being asked to have sex were slim at best.

Half-opened eyes made it hard for Corey to navigate the winding street that ushered motorist into his subdivision. Corey gripped the steering wheel and turned his Audi onto the cul-de-sac where the Grand family's 4,500 square foot mini-mansion postured like a bodybuilder.

Stress lines ran through his forehead the more he struggled to keep his weak arms elevated and maintain a tight grip on the steering wheel. The car's horsepower was real. If he inadvertently tapped the gas pedal too hard the vehicle would buck like an angry bronco.

Corey gave the gas pedal a tap and the engine growled. Moments later, he was coming to a stop inside of his garage. A sigh escaped his mouth while he rested his head on the seat rest.

That girl can suck the chrome off of an Amtrak train, Corey thought. He peeked at the clock on his dashboard. "Corey, you've been gone long enough," he mumbled. "Get your ass inside of this house."

Exhaustion made his legs wiggle like two strings of boiled spaghetti. The tight shoulders that plagued him were a thing of the past. *That young girl is gon' be the death of me,* he thought.

"Bae, I'm home!" Corey called out as he entered the house.

"You don't have to yell. I'm right here."

Eyelids that were drooping seconds earlier sprang open as if someone had attached jumper cables to Corey's lashes.

"Damn, baby." Corey tossed his keys on the countertop, let his gym bag—which doubled as his briefcase on the weekends—fall to the floor, and moved cautiously into the open kitchen space. He looked around as if he was expecting his son to jump out at any moment. "I wasn't expecting you to be standing there. Where is CJ?"

"He's at a play date at the neighbor's house," Rene replied and rested her plump butt on the edge of the kitchen table. She lifted her leg and planted the four-inch Jimmy Choo heel she wore on the seat of the chair. "I know you weren't expecting to see me in this thong, but I decided to surprise you." Rene slid her left hand back on the table and used her elbow to keep her body upright—much like a kickstand on a bike. She used the index finger on her free hand to slide the thin string aside and stuck her finger deep inside of her cavern. "It's been a long time, baby. I'm ready to makeup."

Shit. Shit. Shit. Of all the days on the calendar, she would pick today to wanna fuck. She ain't let me sniff the pussy in weeks and now she wanna get freaky...

"Umm, ummm," Corey stuttered, "let me go get washed up. I'll be back in a minute."

Rene removed her moist finger from between her legs and walked over to Corey. She stuck her finger in his mouth and whispered, "I don't want you to get cleaned up. I want you to come over here and pound this pussy like you've missed it."

The silk robe that clung to her body—her perky breasts being the main reason it didn't fall sooner—fell to the floor. Rene took a few steps backward. Her size Double-D breasts stared at Corey like he owed them money. A belly ring, lodged in the middle of her rippled abdomen, shimmered when hit by the rays of sun that pierced the blinds. Even a blind man could see that Rene's body was every bit as beautiful as Jennifer's. In fact, one could argue that when you factor in the fifteen-year age difference between the women, Rene was the clear winner in the *bangin' body* category.

"Okay, if you're ready then let's take this to the bedroom."

"I'm ready," Rene said. She turned around and placed her elbows on the kitchen table. "But I don't want to go to the bedroom. I want you to fuck me on this table."

"It's like that?"

"Umm hmm," Rene purred and wiggled her hips just enough to make her ass cheeks clap. It was a trick one would never attribute to a woman as sophisticated as Rene, but as she would often say to Corey, 'Just because a woman doesn't walk around actin' like *hoe*, doesn't mean she ain't got a little *hoe* in her.'

Corey wiped the sweat forming on his forehead and closed his eyes.

Lawd, I know I ain't shit. And I know I don't deserve any hookups from you right now. In fact, I know you should probably send my black ass straight to hell for even approaching you after all the shit I've done. But Lawd, ohh Lawd...I need you. I need you right now, Lawd! Pleeeasse Lawd, I promise I won't mess around with Jennifer...

Corey opened one eye and peeked at Rene's clapping ass. Her butt cheeks jostled so violently that for a split second he wondered if she was moonlighting as a stripper when he was out of town on business trips. He closed his eye and finished praying.

...or any other woman out there if you just let my dick get hard. I will even go to counseling to see if I've got an addiction. I promise you I will, Lawd. But I need you to grant me this one prayer. I just need you to touch me, Lawd. Make my dick rise...rise right now, Lawd!

"C'mon, baby," Rene said. She reached back with her right hand and gripped her butt cheek. "I'm so horny; I might let you dig into that other hole you like."

Corey fidgeted like a hooker in church. Scenes from every sexual encounter he'd experienced flashed in his mind.

He grabbed his manhood and stroked harder than a teenage boy taking an extended shower after watching a porn movie.

Rene must have been convinced that Corey would *get it up* because she grabbed the edges of the table and pressed her breasts against it and said, "Come fuck me, baby."

I'm trying to, but this ma'fucka don't wanna cooperate, Corey thought while stretching his dick until it throbbed. He lifted his dick beating hand to wipe his brow again and got a whiff of something. He lowered his hand to within inches of his nostrils.

Shit! My dick still smells like Jennifer's pussy. What if Rene decides she wants to give me some head? I'm gon' be up shit creek. Think fast, think fast, Corey...

"Hold that thought, bae," Corey instructed and moved past Rene, "I've gotta use the bathroom."

"No, baby."

"Bae, you know I can't last if I've gotta pee. Let me take a quick piss and I'll be right out. You stay right there."

"Hurry up."

Corey went into the bathroom and closed the door. He reached underneath the sink and grabbed a hollowed out shaving cream can—the place he kept his Viagra stash.

Yeah buddy. Lawd, since you ain't wanna help a nigga out, I've gotta rely on modern medicine. Corey stared at the plastic baggie he removed from the bottom of the can. There were four oval shaped blue pills in it. *I need this shit to kick in fast so I'm taking two of these ma'fuckas.*

Corey tossed two pills in his mouth, filled his cupped hands with water from the faucet and slurped enough to wash the pills down. He could feel the hairs on the back of his neck dance and wondered if their boogieing was the byproduct of taking two Viagra pills.

"I've gotta wash my dick," he mumbled and flushed the toilet. While the sound of the toilet echoed in the cavernous bathroom, he grabbed a bar of soap, turned on the faucet, and lathered up the towel.

Washing his lover's residue off took seconds, but the erection that arrived would surely last a few hours.

"That's what I'm talkin' 'bout," Corey muttered and watched as his hook grew longer and swayed to the right until the tip tapped him on his abs. "She want this dick, she gon' get this dick."

Corey burst through the bathroom door and into his bedroom like a samurai—his erect penis was his trusty sword. Much to his surprise, Rene was waiting. Corey was about to ask her why she was standing there, but her body language answered the question before it could come fumbling out of his mouth.

Rene's right hand was planted on her protruding hip. Her left leg, which was so long it seemed to start at her shoulder, was extended at a ninety-degree angle. Her curvy silhouette resembled the pointy toe stiletto she wore.

When Corey noticed Rene was wearing her robe his eyebrows bowed and those dancing hairs on his arm stood stiller than wallflowers at a high school dance. He was also curious by the masterful way she twirled another pair of panties like a Hula-Hoop around her left index finger.

"Bae, why are you twirling those panties?" Corey pressed his wrist together and extended his arms toward his sexy wife. He smiled and asked, "What...you wanna tie me up?"

Rene rolled her eyes and in a venomous tone replied, "I should take these panties and choke your black ass!"

"What's wrong?" Corey asked with the shaky voice that often accompanies a guilty conscious.

"These panties were hanging out of your bag...and they ain't mine!"

Not even the double dose of Viagra could keep Corey's penis erect after Rene's announcement.

C'mon Cee, think fast. Stay cool. Don't stutter. Just remain calm and play dumb.

"Huh?" Corey mumbled.

"Huh!" Rene held the panties up like a trophy. "I'm showing you another woman's panties and all you can say is, '*huh*'?"

"You sure those aren't yours?"

"Yeah, I'm sure motherfucker! First of all, they're not my size. Secondly, I don't have that color in my collection. Third, and most important, they stink!" Rene tossed the panties at Corey's mortified looking face. "I hope you wore protection because whoever you're screwing has a funky pussy!"

Corey stood there with a semi-hard dick, wearing another woman's panties on his face like a veil.

Be cool. Don't panic, Corey thought, but his nerves gave his subconscious the middle finger. He did the exact opposite of what his inner voice was telling him to do—he said something stupid.

"C'mon, bae, you're trippin'," Corey uttered clumsily. He sniffed the panties. "First of all, they don't stink. And secondly—"

"Did you just sniff that heifer's panties?"

"Huh?"

"There you go with that '*huh*' shit again," Rene said.

Before Corey could make another stupid comment Rene swung at him. Her fist landed square on Corey's left jaw. Corey didn't fall, but his balance was compromised enough to make him vulnerable to the flurry of blows that followed. Rene wailed on his chest like it was a bass drum.

"I can't believe you're cheating on me," she shouted while landing a stiff jab. "And then you've got the nerve to smell that cow's funky drawers in front of me!"

Corey crouched to protect his face. "You need to calm down! You're the one who threw them in my face!"

"You need to stop being a fucking asshole!"

Determined to not swing back, Corey decided to get Rene off of him with a shoulder blow to her stomach. The force of the blow was enough to make her take a few steps backward.

Corey stood tall and extended his arms. "Baby, I don't wanna hurt you. You need to calm down so we can talk."

Rene grimaced and rubbed her belly for a few seconds. Corey watched her—trying to assess how much physical damage he'd caused.

"Baby, are you okay?"

Rene replied with a head nod. And then without uttering another word she opened up the top drawer and grabbed a t-shirt. She went into the middle drawer and grabbed a pair of jeans.

"Baby, if you give me a second I can explain." Corey took a step forward. When he realized he was still holding the panties he tossed them on the floor. "Ya see, Wayne used that bag last week because his bag got wet—I think he spilled coffee on it or something. Anyway, he asked me if I could loan him something to hold his stuff in." Corey sat on the other side of the bed with his back to Rene. "He must've fucked some chick while he had my bag." Corey sighed and shook his head like he was perplexed by it all. "That nigga always fucking something up; I'ma call 'em and tell 'em to come over here and straighten this shit out."

Corey dug into his pants pocket to grab his phone, but if he'd kept an eye on Rene he would've noticed that she too was reaching for something.

"Yeah, you call Wayne," Rene said from her crouched position. When she stood up she was holding a baseball bat—the one she kept for protection whenever Corey was away on business.

"I'm callin' his ass right now," Corey said and turned on his phone.

"Yeah, you do that," Rene replied calmly. "While you're doing that, I'm gon' be over here proving I can *fuck* some shit up too."

Corey looked back just as Rene was swinging the bat. It didn't hit him, but the edge of the bat came so close to his face that the breeze flirted with his lips.

"I'm gon' kill yo' black ass!" Rene shouted. The swing was forceful enough to make her stagger when the bat came around and rested on her shoulder.

"Girl, what the hell—"

"Ahhh!" Rene yelled and charged at him like an axe wielding murderer in a low budget horror flick.

Corey's fight or flight instincts were summoned. One glimpse at the rage in Rene's eyes helped him make his decision—it was time to flee. But, making it to the door without having the entire left side of his body broken in half by the thirty-two inch wooden Louisville Slugger, was a long shot. Making it to the bathroom was his only option.

Corey lunged toward the bathroom and burst through the door. He managed to close it behind him just as Rene's slender shoulder pounded into it. "Rene, you need to calm down!" A few deep breaths were taken to try to regain his composure. "I told you those panties must be for some chick Wayne is bangin'!"

"Open this damn door!"

"Girl, you're crazier than a ma'fucka if you think I'ma open this door!"

"Well you'd better get used to living in there because I'm gon' be sitting right here waiting for you to come out."

"Well you gon' be sittin' there until you're old and gray because I ain't comin' out until you calm down."

Corey walked over to the tub and sat on the edge of it while he tried to gather his thoughts.

I need assistance. I've gotta get in touch with Wayne and tell him to come over here and help me calm this woman down...

Corey started to dial Wayne's number, but was stopped by the text message from Jennifer that appeared on his screen.

FYI. I think I left my panties somewhere in your office.

Corey damn near broke a fingernail trying to text Jennifer back:

YOU LEFT THEM IN MY BAG! RENE FOUND THEM. SHIT DUN GOT CRAZY OVER HERE!

Corey's heart skipped a beat when he saw the little bubbles pop up on his screen indicating another text message was coming in:

Oops. My bad. Anything I can do?

Did this bitch just say, 'Oops'? Corey thought. He rattled off a response:

YEAH...STAY THE FUCK AWAY!

Nearly a minute elapsed before Jennifer replied:

Okay. I'll hit you in a few days.

This girl clearly doesn't understand English...

DON'T CONTACT ME AGAIN!

Jennifer replied quickly:

Are you serious?

Girl, I ain't got time to have a whole conversation with you...

IS A PIG'S PUSSY PORK? HELL YEAH I'M SERIOUS!

Jennifer replied moments later with the "middle finger" emoji.

Yeah, fuck you too, Corey thought.

Jennifer's hurt feelings were the furthest thing from Corey's mind. He had a crisis on his hands that required his undivided attention.

Corey tip-toed over to the bathroom door and pressed an ear against it. Rene could be heard moving around in the other room. There was a chance he could dart out of the bathroom and make it to the front door, but Rene was fast and she swung that bat like a major league ballplayer—he couldn't risk getting pummeled.

I've gotta get in touch with Wayne.

Corey walked back to the center of the bathroom. He dialed Wayne's number and nearly leapt for joy when he heard his friend's voice.

"What's up?"

"Wayne," Corey whispered, placing his hand over the phone while he spoke, "I need your help, dog."

"Why you whispering?

"Rene found Jennifer's panties."

"She did what?"

"You heard me. She found Jennifer's panties in my bag. Now she got me trapped in the bathroom. She's got a baseball bat waiting for me to come out. I need you to come over here."

"No nigga, you *need* the police."

"C'mon, dog," Corey pleaded.

"What I'm s'posed to do when I get there...take her to the backyard and toss a ball so she can hit it with the bat?"

"I told her the panties belong to a chick you've been fucking."

Wayne laughed.

"This shit ain't funny, dog."

"Yes it is," Wayne said. "You run a multimillion-dollar company, but you ain't the sharpest pencil in the box. That's the best lie you can come up with? Rene knows I'm your best friend. You don't think she knows you're going to give me that charge, and I'm going to back you up?"

"I don't know what the hell she's thinking. I just know I need you to come over here and help me out."

Wayne sighed. "Alright, alright, I'ma come over there, but if she hits me with that bat, I'ma sue the piss outta you."

"Yeah, yeah...just come on over here."

"I'm on my way. In the meantime, I suggest you do what I told you to do the next time that woman catches you with your dick in your hand."

"What?"

"Cop to the lesser charge and give her whatever she wants. I don't care if she wants a goddamn cruise around the world—you'd better open up your checkbook and pay for it."

Corey rubbed his forehead and sat on the edge of the tub. "You're right."

"I'm tellin you, dog—it's your best move. You know Jeffrey Greenburg, the attorney I told you I was hanging out with in Vegas a few months ago?"

"Yeah, what about him?"

"I spoke to him this morning. His divorce was finalized last week. You ready for this?"

"Shoot," Corey mumbled.

"A check for five million dollars. Ten thousand dollars a month child support for one child. And seven thousand dollars a month spousal support for seven years or until she remarries—whichever comes first."

"Damn."

"Damn, is right," Wayne said. "And he ain't worth as much as you. I'm tellin' you—you'd better get on your knees and start kissing some ass. Trust me...it's gon' be cheaper to keep her."

"I hear you," Corey said and sighed. "Just get here as quick as you can."

Corey hung up the phone and pondered Wayne's comments. Stories of men being financially ruined because of divorces were so plentiful that he didn't have to question whether Wayne was exaggerating. Thoughts of being destitute and not being able to see his son on a daily basis swarmed in Corey's head. It was the first time he genuinely feared the outcome of his actions.

Corey moved over to the door and placed his left ear on it again. "Rene, can we talk?"

When Rene didn't respond, Corey pressed his ear against the door harder. That's when he heard a sound that made his heart skip a beat. It was a sound no man ever wants to hear—regardless of how unfaithful he may be—emanating from his wife. Rene was sobbing—uncontrollably.

CHAPTER SIX

Twenty-five minutes later, Corey was alerted to the sound of the doorbell. He felt like a coward for hiding in the bathroom for that long, but he'd rather be a coward with no injuries than a coward with a cracked skull any day. He remained in the bathroom long enough for Rene to answer the door and invite their visitor inside. He approached the bathroom door, listening intently, but their home was far too big for a conversation in the front room to make it all the way back to him.

The reflection in the mirror over the bathroom sink revealed Corey was sweating like a runaway slave. He approached the basin and dried his face with a wash cloth. His eyes were wide with panic when he backed away. His frazzled nerves got another jolt when someone banged on the bathroom door. Every hair on his body stood erect as he spun in that direction.

"You can come out now, you fucking liar."

The voice on the other side of the door was his wife's. Rene didn't sound irate anymore. Her tone was forlorn and exhausted. It sounded like she was all cried out. Corey knew she'd been bawling the whole time it took Wayne to make it to their home. He felt like the worst husband on earth. Rene didn't deserve any of this.

He stared into the mirror again, wondering what the hell was wrong with him. He'd heard about celebrities like Tiger Woods struggling with sex addiction. Corey always thought that was a bullshit diagnosis, but now he wondered if there wasn't something to it. How else could he explain the selfish, irresponsible decisions he'd made? Maybe he'd offer sex addiction as his excuse, if the time came to be honest with Rene. But for now, he felt it was best to stick with his lie, maybe to the bitter end.

Corey unlocked the door and pushed it open cautiously. He found the hallway dark and deserted. He started to peek through the doorway, but there was a chance Rene was waiting to the left or right with her bat. Now that the thought was on his mind, he could picture her standing there, holding her breath, her nostrils flared and her teeth bared, the Louisville Slugger cocked over her shoulder.

Nigga, get a grip on yourself! Corey chided himself. Rene was not going to murder him in cold blood while Wayne waited in the living room.

Maybe not, but Corey brought his forearm up to protect his melon as he stepped out of the bathroom. He looked right and then left. Thankfully his wife was nowhere in sight. He found her in the living room sitting stoically on the loveseat. His best friend Wayne sat on the couch on the opposite side.

They both watched him as Corey walked cautiously into the room. Rene's bat was nowhere in sight, which calmed his nerves considerably. Corey locked eyes with Wayne, and his anxiety eased even more. Without speaking, Corey knew his homey had his back, for better or worse. He

87

took a seat next to Wayne so the two of them could present a united front.

Rene watched the friends closely, her breaths coming slow and hot. Her eyes were red and puffy from crying. Her misery was heart-wrenching, somehow making her appear more beautiful.

Corey started to speak first, but Rene cut him off. She sighed and shook her head before looking Wayne in the eyes.

"My husband's been in the bathroom for a long time. I assume that was long enough for him to fill you in on what's happening here."

Much like her appearance, Rene's voice sounded like all of the fight had been zapped out of her; as if she was merely going through the motions at this point.

"Uh, yeah, he told me a little," Wayne acknowledged. Unable to maintain eye contact with her, he looked uncomfortably at his friend.

Corey half-nodded, his eyes still on his spouse.

"You're gonna tell me you borrowed Corey's bag, and the panties I found tonight belong to one of the hoes you're dating," Rene guessed.

Wayne's eyes swam back in her direction. His jaws clenched for a second before he nodded.

"Yeah, those are mine," he said. "I'm, uh, I'm sorry they caused so much trouble. I can see you're really upset. I apologize for the role I played in this. It's all my fault."

That's what I'm talking about! Corey thought. There weren't too many canines out there who were as loyal as his road dog! If he made it out of this jam, he promised to buy his friend a new Rolex.

"What color are the panties?" Rene asked, her voice still emotionless.

Corey started to speak up, but Rene's eyes became cold when she looked his way. "Keep your mouth shut," she growled.

Corey's jaws snapped closed. He stared at Wayne, hoping he could send the answer to him telepathically.

Wayne shook his head. "Hell, I don't remember. I was more concerned with getting the panties off, than keeping up with what color they were."

Good answer, Corey thought. He started nodding and then caught himself. He didn't want to look like he was cheering his friend on.

"What size does your friend wear?" Rene asked.

Wayne said, "Huh?"

"What size panties?"

Again he shook his head. "Rene, I don't know what size shoes she wears, let alone panties. To be honest, it was just a one-night stand. I don't remember too much about her."

Rene lowered her gaze in disappointment. Corey couldn't tell if she was upset with Wayne for having a one night stand or dismayed because he was backing up Corey's lie. Either way, the conversation was going his way. And for that, Corey was grateful.

"Was she a big girl or a skinny girl?" Rene pressed.

Wayne looked to his friend again and Corey's pulse kicked up a notch. He had told Wayne that Jennifer was fine, with nice hips and a glorious ass, but he wasn't specific about her dimensions. Once again he tried to force the answer into Wayne's head with just his thoughts.

"She, uh, she wasn't too big, and she wasn't skinny either," Wayne said to Rene. "She was average size, I guess..."

Rene brought a hand to her face and rubbed a tense spot on her forehead. "You know," she said, "I expect this kind of shit from my husband, but I thought we were friends." She lowered her hand and looked Wayne in the eyes – hers were filling with tears again.

"You are my friend," Wayne told her.

"How?" she asked. "How am I your friend, if you don't have any respect for me? Do you think sticking up for this asshole makes you a good man? A good friend?"

Wayne wanted to respond to her, but he couldn't find the words.

"You're not being a good friend to me," Rene said. A tear spilled and rolled slowly down her cheek. Her voice rattled when she said, "You're not even being a good friend to Corey right now. A good friend would've told him to stop this foolishness and stop cheating on his wife. A good friend would've told him to man up to his mistakes and take whatever's coming to him. But no, you come over here with your stupid ass *bro-code* and stand up for his trifling ass."

She sniffled and wiped her nose angrily with the back of her hand.

"That's okay," she said, nodding. "You can stick up for him all you want. It doesn't change a goddamned thing, because I know what I know, and you can't bail Corey out this time."

She stood suddenly and stepped to her husband. Despite the fact that she was unarmed and Corey had his friend there for backup, he recoiled slightly.

"We're getting a divorce," Rene announced.

Corey stared up at her in confusion. "Wha, what? But, babe, he just said—"

"I heard what the fuck he said," Rene snarled, "and you heard what the fuck I said."

Corey stood and reached for her. "Babe, you can't leave me for—"

"Get your hands off me," Rene said, snatching her arm away.

"Okay," Corey said, holding his arms to his sides. "But you can't leave me just because you *think* I did something wrong. I'm telling you I didn't do it, and Wayne's sitting right here saying the same thing. What are you gonna divorce me for?"

"You can take that tired ass story to court if you want to," Rene replied. "We'll see who the judge believes."

"You're being silly," Corey said. "We'll talk about this later."

"Yeah, whatever," Rene said. "And if you care anything about that nasty-ass dick of yours, don't even think about climbing into bed with me tonight. I swear to God you won't have it when you wake up."

She stared him down for a few seconds before turning and leaving the room. Corey blew out a pent up breath and then checked to see how his friend was holding up. He could tell Wayne had something he wanted to say. Thankfully he waited until Corey walked him outside before speaking his mind.

"Man, that was some fucked up shit," Wayne said.

Corey nodded as they stepped off the porch. Without thinking, he pulled half a pack of cigarettes from his pocket and lit one up. Wayne frowned as he watched him.

"You smoking again?"

"Just a little bit," Corey responded.

"I told you not to fuck around with that hoe," Wayne said, his voice lowered. "You called me and asked for my advice. I told you flat out not to do it. Your dumb ass must've hung up with me and called her right over."

Corey didn't bother denying that. He looked back to make sure the front door was closed and then turned away from his friend before blowing out a chest full of smoke.

"And now you got Rene thinking I'm just as bad as you," Wayne complained.

"So what?" Corey said. "Why does it matter if she thinks that?"

"I like Rene. I considered her a friend, but now that's gone."

"Once again, so what?" Corey said. "You're not the one who could end up in divorce court over this. What do you stand to lose? *A friend*? You got plenty of friends. And I'm sure Rene will forgive you once we get past this."

"Naw." Wayne shook his head knowingly. "Even if she does end up forgiving you – *again* – she'll never like me again. She'll cut her eyes every time we're around each other."

Corey took another drag and blew it out slowly. "Once again, *so what*? I would do the same for you if any of your girlfriends ever accused you of something."

"It ain't the same," Wayne grunted. "My girlfriends come and go. Rene's here for the long haul."

"Alright, I'm sorry," Corey replied. "I didn't know you valued your friendship with her more than your friendship with me."

"It ain't about who I'm more friends with."

"Yes, that's exactly what it's about," Corey stated. "You're *my* homeboy. You're only her friend by extension.

So please get off this corny ass shit. I was thinking about buying you a Rolex, if you managed to save my marriage tonight."

"A Rolex?"

"Yeah," Corey said, patting him on the back. "You did your thing tonight. I don't think I can thank you enough."

"I'll take the *Roley*," Wayne replied. "But for real man, if you manage to keep Rene after this shit, you're a fool if you ever cheat again. You got a good woman, and you know what's at stake if she divorces you. I'm telling you, dog, PornHub is way better than what you're going through."

"I think I got a sex addiction," Corey revealed. "I was thinking about that while I was waiting for you to get here."

"Get the fuck outta here with that. Ain't no such thing as a *sex addiction*. Your ass is just horny."

"But what about Tiger Woods and Eric Benet and them?"

"They're just some rich ass freaks," Wayne said. "Just like you."

Corey considered that but wasn't sure if he agreed with him. "Alright, man. Thanks again for coming over. I'ma hook you up, bro. I promise."

"You bet not give me no knock off," Wayne said as he opened his car door. "I know a real *Roley* when I see one."

Corey chuckled nervously and smoked the rest of his cigarette as his friend rolled out of the circular drive.

The next few days were reminiscent of the time that passed after the initial "Babysittergate" scandal. The only difference was Rene was more resolved with her beliefs and her plans. She didn't speak to Corey at all on day one, and he avoided communicating with her as well. He heard her on the phone with friends a few times. The "D" word was a recurring theme in her conversations. Corey didn't think she'd really try to divorce him, but he dug through his file cabinet anyway, searching for a copy of their prenuptial agreement.

As he recalled, the contract rewarded her handsomely if Corey was the one who initiated a divorce. But Rene would get the short end of the stick if she wanted to end the marriage. The only exception to this was if she could prove he committed adultery.

True, she'd caught him cheating in the past. But since she didn't pursue a divorce then, it was almost as if those incidents never happened. As far as his latest transgression, Corey knew she couldn't win a favorable divorce settlement based on a random pair of panties, so he wasn't worried too much about her silent treatment or her friends goading her into doing something drastic.

On day two Rene came to the guest bedroom where Corey had been sleeping and initiated a conversation. He was startled when he woke up and saw her standing there, but he sat up casually and appeared unbothered. He knew everything she'd accused him of was spot-on, but he also knew her smoking gun lacked definitive proof of an affair. He stared at her lazily, waiting for her to speak her mind.

She took a seat at the desk and turned the swivel chair toward him. "Have you thought about what we talked about?"

Corey watched her for a few seconds before saying, "We haven't really talked, Rene. You said you wanted to get a divorce. That's not a conversation. That's you yelling at me."

"You're right," she agreed. "But have you thought about it?"

He nodded. "Yeah, I thought about it. And I contacted my lawyer." That was a bluff. Corey hoped to gauge his wife's reaction, but she surprised him by not having one. "Lawyer says our prenup will stand up in court, and it'll benefit me," Corey went on. "If you divorce me for no reason, you leave with whatever you brought into the marriage – which is pretty much nothing."

"Really?" Rene said, cocking her head slowly. "*My* lawyer says if I leave you because of *adultery*, I get half of everything; the business, the accounts, retirement funds. *Everything*."

Corey's heart froze and sank to his belly like a boulder. She had outplayed him. He wasn't sure if she had really contacted an attorney, but her response got a rise out of him. He wasn't able to hide his reaction as well as she had.

"But you can't prove adultery," he said, hoping his voice remained steady, though every other part of his body felt sickly.

"Oh?" she said. "I can't?"

Corey swallowed. Did she know something he didn't? He didn't think his wife was anywhere near as cunning as he was.

"A random pair of panties doesn't prove anything," he replied. "Wayne already told you they were his – I mean they were his girlfriend's. If I gotta drag Wayne to court to testify, you know he'll do it."

Rene nodded and smiled smugly. The termites eating away at Corey's certainty kicked into overdrive. He could almost feel their sharp, little teeth digging into his brain.

"Unless Wayne's dating *Jennifer*, he was lying about whose panties those are," Rene said.

Corey's eyes widened. A dark chill rolled down his spine, but her comment actually made him feel better about the way this little talk was going. He allowed an arrogant grin to brighten his features.

"Really, baby? *Jennifer*? We're going back to that?"

Rene's upbeat expression did not fade. "You're the one who went back to that, darling."

"We've been through this," Corey said. "I told you I never grabbed her ass. Are you so paranoid you can't let it go? Are you gonna bring her up every time you feel unsure about something I'm doing?"

She shook her head. "No, dear. I'm bringing her up because I know those are her panties. But, like I said, if you wanna deny it, you can tell your side of the story to the judge." Rene rose to her feet but didn't leave the room before delivering a parting shot. "We're getting a divorce. I can prove you committed adultery, and I'm taking half of everything. I'm moving back to California, and you best believe CJ's coming with me."

"You're out of your mind, if you think any of that is happening," Corey said.

Rene exited the room as if she didn't hear him.

Ten minutes later, Corey stood in the backyard, spraying water on their glorious garden. It was a beautiful day; bright, cottony clouds in the sky. But Corey only saw gloom and doom as he kept an eye on the back door. Unless Rene left the house through the front and entered the backyard via the side gate, he would see her approaching long before she saw him. It was still risky to call Jennifer while Rene and CJ were home, but Corey would have no peace of mind until he spoke to his mistress.

He *hotboxed* the last cigarette in his pack while he waited for Jennifer to answer the phone. He couldn't believe he'd smoked twenty cigarettes in just two weeks. Compared to the habit he had before quitting, that didn't sound so bad. But when he purchased the pack, he thought it would last him a couple of months. Now he was craving nicotine so badly, he planned to buy more the moment he got off the phone.

Corey thought his call was going to voicemail, but Jennifer answered after five agonizingly long rings.

"Hello?"

Corey was sure no one inside the house could hear him, but he kept his voice low just the same. "What you doing?"

"Chilling," Jennifer said. "Surprised to hear from you."

"Oh yeah. And why is that?"

"The last time we spoke, you told me not to contact you again. I asked if you were sure, and you said something about a pig's pussy."

At any other time, her response would've been comical. But Corey's funny bone had been disabled.

"Listen," he said with a sigh, "Rene's trippin' again. She brought your name up."

After a pause, Jennifer said, "What do you mean?"

"She's convinced those were your panties she found the other day. She said she can prove we slept together."

"How? Why does she think that?"

"I don't know," Corey replied. "As far as I can tell, she's got it out for you. She hasn't let go of that booty grab incident, and she's trying to put the pieces together. But I told her just because she *thinks* those are your panties doesn't mean she can prove it."

"That's right," Jennifer said. "Those panties could belong to anybody. Wait – does she still have them? You think she'd go as far as looking for DNA?"

"To be honest, I wouldn't put anything past her at this point," Corey said. "But, no, she doesn't have them. I told her they belonged to one of my homeboy's girlfriends, and I made him take 'em with him when he came over."

"Good. Then your wife doesn't have anything on you."

"She doesn't as long as you stick to the script," Corey said. "You're the only one who can ruin this for me."

"Oh, so now you need me? The other day you were talking shit, didn't want nothing to do with me."

"Hey, I'm not playing around," Corey breathed. "This ain't no game. She's talking about divorce, calling lawyers and shit. That booty grab is *nothing* compared to what's happening now."

"Alright. Alright. I was just kidding."

"This ain't no time for that. I need to know that you got my back. I could lose everything, if you decide to start talking about what we got going on."

Corey regretted his words the moment they left his lips.

"Everything, huh?" Jennifer said.

He could hear her smiling over the phone.

"Must be worth something to not lose *everything*," she went on.

He gritted his teeth and blew hot fumes from his nostrils.

"Alright, what the fuck you want?" he asked.

"Baby, you don't have to come at me like that," Jennifer said with a chuckle. "I would never blackmail you."

"Mmmm hmmm."

"I mean, if you happen to find it in your heart to buy me a few Birkin bags..."

This bitch, Corey thought. She wasn't blackmailing him, but she wanted a few Birkin bags. Those purses cost up to twenty thousand or more – *apiece*! No pussy was worth that much. But to save his fortune, Corey would shell out the hush money. Compared to all he had to lose, Jennifer's request was a mere pittance.

Even still, he wondered if he could hire a hit man for less than that. He quickly pushed the thought out of his mind. He may have been a no-good, low-down, dirty dog, but Corey was certainly no killer.

"If this all goes away, and we don't get a divorce, I'll buy you a fucking Birkin," he told her.

"I said *bags*," Jennifer corrected him. "That means *plural*."

"Alright, bitch. But you better make sure your lips remain sealed. I'm talking tight like super glue."

"Okay, daddy. Give me a call when all of this blows over."

Corey knew he couldn't respond without cursing her out, so he simply disconnected.

On Monday, Corey awakened confident and refreshed, despite the fact that he'd spent another night in his guest bedroom. Rene didn't speak to him when he entered the bedroom to pick out an outfit for work, but CJ still had plenty of love for his dad. Corey knew his son was affected by the turmoil in their home, but it would all be over soon.

If Rene was foolish enough to file for divorce with no evidence of adultery, she'd be the big loser when it was all said and done. Once she had a good sit-down with her lawyer, if she really had one, she'd realize the error of her ways and back down. It might take a while for things to go back to normal at home, but Corey was confident everything would settle down with time. He'd stop cheating, *maybe*, and everyone would live happily ever after.

CJ chatted incessantly and followed Corey around the bedroom while he tried to get dressed for work. Corey really didn't have the time to entertain him, but after receiving a cold shoulder all weekend, it felt good to talk to *someone*.

"Don't go to work, Daddy," CJ called as he followed Corey to the garage. "Stay here with me and mama."

Corey felt guilty, so he knelt and looked his son in the eyes. He smiled at what was clearly a younger version of himself. "I gotta go to work. Who do you think pays all the bills around here?"

"You don't have to pay the bills," CJ complained. "I'll pay the bills for you."

"Oh really? And how are you gonna do that?"

"With my allowance."

Corey laughed. "Alright. When the electric bill comes next month, I'll let you take care of it."

CJ nodded, grinning proudly. "Okay."

"But until then, I gotta go to work," Corey said, rising to his full height. "Now go inside. You know I don't want you in the garage when I'm coming or going."

The boy pouted but was obedient to his father.

When Corey got to the office, he hit the ground running. The stress from the weekend quickly melted away as he threw himself into his work and made gains for his investors. His troubles at home were all but forgotten until he got a call on his cellphone. He stared at the display in confusion when he saw his wife's name on the Caller ID.

He accepted her call with a gruff, "Yeah."

"Soooo, I sent you proof of your adultery," Rene informed him. "Did you get it yet?"

"What? Woman, what the hell are you talking about?"

As he spoke, Corey's cellphone vibrated in his hand. The vibration was accompanied by a notification chime he recognized as Facebook Messenger. He pulled the phone away from his face, and sure enough, there was a bubble on the screen with his wife's image on it.

"What is this?" he asked as he tapped the icon.

The application opened, and Corey saw the video Rene had sent him. He knew his whole world had come to an end before he even opened it. The screenshot was so damning, he nearly lost his breakfast. He felt like every organ in his body had shut down simultaneously.

He was so shaken that his finger didn't register enough heat to click the video when he tapped his phone. He had to try several times before the clip began to play.

101

What he saw caused the contents of his stomach to rumble again. This time the back of his throat burned with gastric acid. Corey swallowed it down as he stared at something so deplorable, he felt like he was having an out of body experience.

Rene wasn't bluffing. The video depicted enough adultery to bury Corey in a court of law. He saw himself ramming Jennifer, long and hard, as she scrambled atop his desk, reaching for something to hold onto. The video quality was excellent. Corey hadn't turned off the lights during their last rendezvous because he loved to see everything. Now he saw much more than he ever wanted to.

The thought of Rene watching the video rocked him to the core. The only saving grace was the audio on the video was disabled due to the fact that he was on the phone. He could only imagine what he'd hear when he viewed it again after Rene hung up.

Corey couldn't breathe. He couldn't move either, but he had to. He broke free of the paralysis and shot to his feet. He scanned the room, attempting to calculate the angle the video was shot from. There were no security cameras in his office, so he knew he'd been recorded surreptitiously. Somehow, someone had planted a device in the room. But, for the life of him, Corey couldn't locate it. Everything in his office looked the same as it always had.

Dear God, was she watching him now??

Corey lurched back to his seat as the video ended. He sat down slowly, the ruins of his life flashing before his eyes. She had him. Some way, somehow, Rene had finally got the upper hand.

Corey's mouth was so dry, he sounded like he was dying of thirst when he asked her, "What do you want?"

When Rene responded, she had the air of a confident woman; a woman who knew she was in complete control.

"You know, Corey, when I first found out about this affair, I wanted to kill you – you and Jennifer. How could you? You grabbed that heifer's ass in our home – in front of CJ! Both of you have been lying to me like it ain't nothing. I wanted you *dead*, Corey. I wanted you dead for all the times you did this to me and I didn't find out about it."

Corey didn't know what to say about that, so he remained silent.

"And then," Rene went on, "I decided it would be fun to ruin you, take half of everything you have. But the more I thought about it, the more I realized that wouldn't really ruin you. If you've got 20 million in assets, and I get half, you'll still have ten million. Even if I get two-thirds, you're still a fucking millionaire. You could dissolve *our* company and live on a resort for the rest of your life."

Corey couldn't deny any of that was true. Rene hadn't asked him to respond, so he kept his mouth closed and let her vent.

"What I finally decided," she said, "is to get you back in a way that will hurt you, like *real deep*. I know I could take CJ away from you, but I don't want to punish our son in the process. For whatever reason, he loves your stupid ass. I'm pissed, but I'm not cruel enough to deny a child his father."

Corey was relieved to hear that, but he didn't take a moment to appreciate her concession. Rene still hadn't said what she wanted, and from the sound of it, it was something he wouldn't like. Nope, not one bit.

"Get to the point, Rene. What do you want?"

"I wanna have a threesome," she blurted out.

Out of all the things she could've requested, a threesome wasn't on Corey's radar. "*What?*"

"You heard me. I want you to watch another man fuck me," she said. "Of course it's a *threesome*, so you'll be involved in the fun too. But I think being forced to share me with another man is a fitting punishment for you – since I had to share you with that bitch, Jennifer."

Corey blinked quickly, not sure how to respond. Rene's request was outlandish. He thought he'd rather go through with a divorce than even consider it.

"You wanna have a threesome with who?"

"I want the threesome with *Wayne*," she revealed. "Since you two are always there for each other, he should be the one to fuck your wife. Maybe after I suck his dick, you'll appreciate what I have to offer and cut all your little hoes off."

Corey felt worse than he did when he watched the video she sent him. The things she was saying were disgusting. There was no way on God's green earth he'd let Wayne tap his wife. Fuck that. It wasn't happening.

"It's either that or a divorce," Rene said, as if reading his mind. "Think about seeing your son every other weekend before you decide. It's Monday... You've got exactly one week to make up your mind."

She hung up and left Corey to ponder his infidelities and her *indecent* proposal. He thought he'd gotten over his bout of nausea. No such luck. He dropped his phone and snatched the wastebasket from beneath his desk just as all of the guilt, panic, and disgust came rumbling up his esophagus.

CHAPTER SEVEN

The remnants of the previous night's dinner and the wine used to wash the meal down stained Corey's tongue. A sewer-like stench clung to his taste buds and a comparable odor came from the tiny trashcan next to his desk.

Corey gathered the small garbage bag that lined his wastebasket and tied a knot in the top. With his left hand gripping the puke bag and his right index finger pressing the intercom button on his desk phone Corey called out, "Carol!"

"Yes, Mr. Grand."

"Do we have any small wastebasket bags?"

"The cleaning crew left us some. I'll bring one to you."

"Thank you."

Carol Indigo, fifty-eight, a widow, and devoid of a funny bone, had been with Corey since he started his company a decade earlier. She was loyal, prompt, respectful, and professional—almost to the point of being overbearing. She never referred to Corey by his first name and never used profanity. She avoided religious conversations in the workplace, but it was clear she was a devout Christian by the conservative way she spoke, dressed, wore her hair in a tight bun, and often read a tiny King James version of the Bible at her desk during her lunch breaks.

"I brought two," Carol said as she entered his office with the bags flapping in the wind. "You can put the extra bag at the bottom of the basket so you'll have it when you need it."

"Thanks, Carol," Corey said and stood up. "I'm glad you brought two bags because I need that second bag to place this nasty one in."

"What happened?"

"Must've been something I ate," Corey said and shoved the vomit filled bag inside of one of the new bags Carol gave him. He tied a knot in the new bag. "Thanks. I'm gon' go throw this in the dumpster out back."

"You won't do no such thing," Carol said and reached for the bag. "Give it to me, I'll take it out back. You need to get prepared for your meeting this morning."

"Meeting?" Corey asked quizzically.

"Yes, sir," Carol said as she spun on her heels—arm extended to keep the bag away from her body—and walked toward the door. "You have a meeting in thirty minutes with Tony Espinoza. I gave you a breakdown of his company last week. Did you study it?"

"No, I was too busy, and I didn't get a chance to come in this weekend to study it."

"Well you'd better start cramming. The file is in the top file drawer."

Corey waited until Carol closed his office door before he reacted to her reminder.

"Shit! Shit! Shit!" He moved quickly over to a file cabinet in the corner of his office and pulled out a burgundy folder. He peeked over at the clock on his wall. *I've got about fifteen minutes to learn everything about this man's company.*

Corey's personal life was so chaotic that he'd forgotten about his meeting with Tony Espinoza, CEO/President of Espinoza Mexican Grill. With seventeen locations scattered throughout the Dallas/Fort Worth area, each more than three thousand square feet, this was the type of steady "mom and pop" client every security company loves to have in its portfolio.

A little country club gossip gave Corey what he perceived to be an inside track to landing the contract. Word on the links was Tony Espinoza was trying to receive financing to build another dozen restaurants, and locate them in the Houston and San Antonio markets. Landing this account would be a major feather in Corey's hat and position Grand Security for growth into southern Texas.

Corey studied the Espinoza file like a college student cramming for an exam. If it weren't for his decision to follow his *little* head instead of the *big* one on his shoulder, he could've knocked out his client research over the weekend. But, the only thing he had his head buried in was Jennifer's vagina.

Carol used her tiny knuckles to rap on Corey's office door before she opened it. "Mr. Grand, can I come in?"

Corey motioned for her to enter without looking up.

"Mr. Espinoza is in the lobby," Carol whispered.

Corey glanced at his watch. "Damn, he's prompt."

"And he's also a strict Christian," Carol said. "He doesn't curse so try to watch your language."

Carol's tone hovered somewhere between admonishing and informative.

"How do you know all of that?"

"We attend the same church. His wife stands next to me in the choir." Carol leaned forward and whispered in an even lower voice. "So be on your best behavior."

"I thought Mr. Espinoza sought me out on his own."

"He did," Carol said with a sly grin, "after I planted the seed in his wife's ear at choir rehearsal last month." She turned and moved toward the door. "I'll give you five minutes to get yourself together. At the top of the hour press the intercom button on your phone to make it squelch—that'll be my signal that you're ready."

Corey looked astonished. Carol worked as his Administrative Assistant for ten years and this was the most personality he could ever recall her showing.

"Thanks, Carol."

"You've got your flaws, but I like you," Carol said and smiled. "You've always done right by me so this is the least I can do for you. I just got him here," she pointed at Corey, "but you've gotta close the deal." She pointed at his bathroom. "Now hurry up and brush your teeth, wash your face," she pointed at his desk, "and pop a mint in your mouth."

Corey smiled when he saw the pack of Mentos next to the marble nameplate. "Carol," he said and stood up, "that was smooth."

Carol winked and exited the room. Corey followed her instructions to a tee and returned to his desk just as the clock struck ten. He pressed the intercom button to signal to Carol he was ready and took a deep breath.

"Mr. Grand," Carol said as she opened the officer door seconds later, "this is Mr. Tony Espinoza."

"Good morning, Mr. Espinoza," Corey said as he moved from behind his desk and shook his visitor's hand.

Tony Espinoza would have struggled to reach five-eight if he stood on top of an oil barrel. With a receding hairline and a midsection that suggested he'd taste tested one too many of his restaurant's calorie filled dishes, he was anything but intimidating. But what he lacked in physical stature he more than made up for with his reputation for being a shrewd businessman.

Carol passed Espinoza off to Corey the way a sprinter passes the baton in a relay race. She did an about-face and left the two moguls alone.

"Thank you for taking time to meet with me, Mr. Grand."

"It's an honor," Corey replied. "I've watched your empire grow from afar over the years. In fact, my wife and I went to your restaurant on Beltline for our first date."

"You mean the one near here?"

"Yes, sir. The one near Royal and Beltline."

"That's one of my favorites," Espinoza said and smiled proudly. "It was our first so it has a special place in my heart."

"You should be very proud."

"And so should you," Espinoza said and looked around Corey's office. "I did a little research on your company too. You have been growing faster than many of your competitors."

Corey's nod reflected his own sense of pride. "Thank you." He moved back around his desk and sat down in his chair. "It hasn't always been easy. We've had some tough times, but we made it through so I won't complain."

"I understand, trust me." Espinoza nodded and looked at the tips of his buffed shoes. "I'm going through one of those tough times right now. That's why I'm here today."

Corey placed his forearms and elbows on his desk and leaned forward. He interlocked his fingers and studied the intriguing man. "What's your problem Mr. Espinoza and how can I help?"

"Please, call me Tony."

"Okay, Tony. You can call me, Corey." Corey leaned back in his chair. "I couldn't help but notice the stressed look on your face when you said the words *tough times*. How can I help you, Tony?"

"Well, it isn't public knowledge yet, but my company is about to expand into southern Texas."

Dude your business is more public than you think. I've been hearing about that for two months. I even know what bank you're using to finance your loan...

"I didn't know that," Corey lied, "congratulations!"

"Thank you. We've been keeping it pretty hush...don't want the competition to know my plans and beat me to the punch."

Too late for that homeboy...

"Wise move. You don't want the competition stealing your thunder."

"Agreed. But it's not the competition that I'm worried about ruining this for me. It's crime."

Corey leaned forward again. "What do you mean?"

"In 2016, three of my stores were robbed. So far this year, two of my stores have been robbed—including the one you took your wife to on your first date."

"I'm sorry to hear that."

"Thanks. Well, now my insurance carrier is threatening to raise my rates to some ridiculous amount."

"Change carriers."

"That would be more expensive. I have a twenty-year relationship with my current carrier. A new insurance carrier would dig deeper into my business closet—explore things that my current carrier turns a blind eye to...if you know what I mean."

Corey nodded. "Understood."

"Good. So you understand my concerns about dealing with a new insurance company. But, there are headaches associated with staying with my new company. A new policy would be more expensive, and require me to go back to the bank that's financing my expansion and try to get more money."

"Which leads to a higher interest rate," Corey said.

"Exactly!"

"Are these robberies the work of one person or are they separate incidents?"

"The police don't know. They say it could be random or the work of a team that's targeting my restaurants. What I do know is that my insurance carrier has given me an ultimatum; either increase the physical security at my restaurants or deal with higher premiums."

"Putting an armed officer at fifteen restaurants—"

"Seventeen," Espinoza corrected him.

"Excuse me," Corey said. "An armed guard at seventeen restaurants for eight hours—because you're going to want the officer to be there for a few hours after closing to protect your manager when he or she is transferring money to the bank—can be expensive."

"I understand that, but the cost of a security guard is nothing compared to the cost of insurance premiums and bad publicity. I can't afford to let some hoodlums ruin this for me."

"I understand."

"Can your company handle the job?"

"My company can handle your Dallas restaurants and the restaurants in southern Texas once you expand."

"That's the plan."

The two men shook hands. When they released each other's hand, Espinoza raised his index finger to the sky.

"I do have one stipulation, Corey."

"What's that?"

"I'm sure Carol told you that she and I attend the same church."

"Yes, she told me that today."

"She's good friends with my wife. That's how I learned of your company. I'd heard of your company before, but I never knew that someone who was friends with my wife worked for you. It's like God sent you to me in my time of need."

"Praise God," Corey said, knowing he only called on God in times of need—as was the case that past weekend. But if it improved his chances of getting the contract he intended to milk the Christian angle for all it was worth. "God is good."

"Yes, he is. Are you a Christian, Corey?"

Man, I can't remember the last time I went to church...

"Yes, sir," Corey said, nearly shouting. "My wife and I attend a church near our home."

"That's good to know because I make no secret about my desire to do business with other Christians. Especially other Christians who are minorities." Espinoza stood up and stuck out his hand to shake Corey's again. "The fact that you are a family man and you spend time with your wife in church is impressive. I respect that." He squeezed Corey's hand tighter. "I suspect this is the beginning of a long...and prosperous...business relationship."

Espinoza released his grip and walked toward the door. "I'll leave my information with Carol. I'll have my assistant send you the specs, you can use them to come up with your rate, and send the figures to me. I'm scheduled to meet with the president of the insurance company in two weeks so I'd really like to be able to give him a detailed security plan when we meet. If you could have your quote to me by this time next week I'd appreciate it."

"You'll have it before then."

Corey watched his door close behind the Hispanic multi-millionaire, and then immediately started crunching the numbers in his head.

One armed guard per restaurant. Eight hours a day. Six days a week. At twenty-five dollars an hour. For fifty-two weeks a year. Shit...this is going to be a million dollar contract. And that's before he expands to southern Texas.

Corey smiled and started rubbing his palms together. But that smile faded once he remembered Espinoza's emphasis on marriage.

Shit! If he finds out I may be going through a divorce because of my adulterous behavior that could ruin everything.

The middle and index fingers on both hands were used to rub his temples.

If Rene finds out about this deal and this man's emphasis on marriage, she's going to really have me by the balls.

Corey slammed his fist down on the arm of his chair.

I never thought I'd say this...but I may actually have to follow Wayne's advice and give her what she wants.

Corey stared at the phone on his desk. Rene's demand qualified as *over the top*, but the thought of not seeing his son for months at a time terrified him. That terror was doubled by the realization that he'd probably be forced to part ways with more than half of everything he'd worked so hard to attain.

And then there was the Espinoza deal. Grand Security stood to make the kind of money and connections that would take Corey's empire to the next level. All he had to do to keep his child, money, and ensure the growth of his company, was to agree to let his wife have sex with his best friend.

The universe can be cruel. And Karma can be a certified bitch, Corey thought.

While Corey struggled with whether or not to give in to Rene's demands, his cell phone started squealing like it was being tortured. He rolled his eyes when he saw the name of the caller on the phone screen—Wayne.

"Hello," Corey said.

"Damn, dog. You sound like someone just stole your wallet."

You're joking, but you're closer to the truth than you realize, Corey thought. "I'm cool. What's up?"

"Just checking on you, dog. You alright?"

"No," Corey said and rubbed his temple, "I'm fucked up right now."

"What's goin' on?"

"I can't get into it right now. Let's play a round this Saturday. I'll run it all down to you on the golf course."

"You sure you wanna wait? I'm shutting it down early today. We can go have some drinks at this new bar in Addison I've been hearing about. First round is on me."

"I'll pass. I need to get my mind right. Set up a tee time for Saturday morning."

"Say no more, playa. I'm on it."

"Peace," Corey said.

"Keep your head up, playa. You gon' be alright."

Corey wasn't as confident as Wayne that everything was going to work out fine, but he was hoping his friend was right. His pensive mood was booted by his curiosity.

"I'm sitting here thinking about what to do, but what I should be doing is trying to figure out how that damn video got recorded."

Corey sprang from his chair like a meerkat sensing danger. He turned on his cell phone and reopened the video Rene sent.

"This video is steady," he mumbled. "Too steady for someone to be holding the camera."

Corey cocked his head. His nervous eyes kept jumping from the screen to his office and back to his screen until he was able to pinpoint the exact spot where the camera must've been positioned.

"It had to be positioned right here," he said out loud and pointed at a spot in the furthest corner from where he and Jennifer had sex. He walked over to the spot. "I'll be damn," he muttered and moved the leaves of a huge potted plant that stood around five feet high. The leaves were large enough to fan a human with. "Whoever set this camera up over here not only knew I wouldn't be able to see it while it recorded, but also knew I would never wander over here long enough to spot it before or after the recording."

Anger rose in Corey's gut and plummeted down to his feet. He kicked the porcelain pot that held the plant upright so hard it cracked like an egg.

"Is everything alright in here?" Carol asked as she burst through the door.

"Carol, when was the last time the cleaning staff came in here?"

"They normally come in on Saturday's."

Corey wanted to refute that, but to do so would be an admittance that he'd lied about coming into the office on Saturday.

"Do you know if they came this Saturday?"

"I'm sure they did. We've used them for two years and they've never missed a weekend. No one from their office said they weren't coming so I assume they did. What's wrong? Do you think someone stole something from your office?"

"No." Corey put his phone in the inside pocket of his suit coat. "Find a new company to do our housekeeping."

"I don't understand, Mr. Grand. What happened?"

"Just do it!"

Carol lurched back. Corey had never used that type of tone with her and the look on her face showed she was clearly taken aback. "Yes, sir," she muttered. "I'll contact their office right away and let them know their services are no longer needed. Do you care that there may be some type of cost associated with ending the contract?"

116

"No," Corey said. He plopped down in his chair and buried his face in his hands. His voice was muffled while he spoke from that point on, but he had no problem getting his message across to his trusty sidekick. "I don't care what it cost. I just don't want anyone representing that company back in this building."

Moments after Carol closed the door Corey lifted his head. He squinted as his thoughts raced around his mind.

What if it wasn't the housekeeping crew? What if Rene set up the video? But how could she have done that? When I got to the house she was there waiting for me in a thong. There is no way in hell she would've been ready for sex if she knew I'd just had sex.

Corey opened his desk drawer and removed a bottle of Tylenol. The tiny refrigerator he kept behind his desk had one bottle of water left in it. After washing down three 500mg pills he sat back and thought some more.

Maybe it was Jennifer. Maybe she recorded us having sex. Corey pulled his phone out and started texting.

RENE HAS A VIDEO OF US HAVING SEX. WHY DID YOU DO THAT 2 ME?

It took Jennifer nearly ten minutes to respond...

I don't know anything about a video.

Corey knew she would deny it so he already had his response cued up...

STOP LYING! HOW ELSE WOULD SHE GET A TAPE OF US FROM THIS PAST WEEKEND?

Being accused of lying was enough to stoke the ire of the normally laid back vixen...

Corey, I don't know. You begged me to come over there to see you, remember? Maybe those housekeepers you're always talking about overhearing us recorded it. Stop texting me with this bullshit. I'm tired of being in you and your wife's mess. If you're that damn paranoid maybe y'all should get a divorce. Figure it out and leave me alone.

Corey's fingers went to work, but he stopped typing halfway through his sentence. Jennifer would never confess to being the culprit so badgering her was a waste of time. Besides that, he struggled to understand what her motive would be. If she wanted to cause problems for him she could've done that sooner. He'd already agreed to her blackmail demands so there would've been no need for her to sabotage her own victory.

Corey deleted the message he was about to send and tossed the phone on his desk. He spun around in his chair and stared out the window. His facial features were placid, but inside of his chest, emotions were scampering like a duck's webbed feet underneath the surface of a pond.

"Mr. Grand," Carol said as she entered.

"Yes," Corey replied without turning around.

"I contacted the cleaning company and let them know that we no longer needed them. I've identified three other companies we can use. Would you like to go over them now or later?"

"Later," Corey said. "Oh...and Carol."

"Yes, sir."

Corey's chair turned around. "I apologize for raising my voice."

"That's okay. As long as I've worked here you've never raised your voice at me so I know whatever it is that's bothering you must be serious. I'll be praying for your peace of mind."

Carol closed the door. Corey turned back around in his chair and stared out his office window again.

Yeah, pray for me. Because I am fucked.

Saturday morning came faster than Corey would have liked. He and Rene spent the entire week treating each other as if they were invisible. Every time he walked past her in the house he hoped she'd stop him and rescind the indecent proposal. But that never happened. In fact, Rene's disposition bordered on smug—like someone playing *Spades* holding both jokers and the ace of spades.

Corey tried to combat Rene's arrogance with a little haughtiness of his own. He laughed and played with CJ like nothing was bothering him. All the while, he could feel his organs shriveling—being emasculated can have that effect.

Corey arrived at the club before Wayne, and as usual, Wayne pulled up late making a lot of noise.

"What's up, dog!" Wayne shouted in his usual care free tone as he pulled his clubs out of his trunk. "I'm feeling good today. I'm gon' beat you like you stole something."

Corey, usually eager to engage in a little innocent trash talk, remained quiet. He sat on the golf cart next to his chipper friend and stared out at the manicured golf course.

"Dude, that woman has you shook," Wayne teased. "If you'd stop being stubborn and shower her with gifts she'd be okay."

"It ain't that simple," Corey muttered.

"It is that simple," Wayne fired back. "Rene may be mad, but she ain't stupid. Let's look at her options...she could stay with you—"

"Or she could divorce me and take half of everything I own."

"She ain't gon' do that," Wayne said, while he shook his head and swatted away Corey's comment.

"How do you know?"

"Because I know women." Wayne looked Corey dead in the eyes. "Listen up grasshopper, you might learn somethin'."

"I'm listenin'."

"Dog, Rene knows she won't find another brotha that's got as much going for himself as you do. I don't care how many of those bullshit dating sites she goes on; most of the dudes on those sites are just saying whatever they need to say to get some pussy. Trust me, I know."

"And how do you know that?"

"Nigga, I've got a profile on every one of those sites. I tell them bitches whatever they wanna hear, get the drawers, and don't call their asses again. Those sites are like a playa's playground." Wayne laughed at his own joke. "Look, bruh...

Rene has become used to a certain lifestyle, and I don't care what anybody says, no woman wants to take a step backward in the *lifestyle* department. Did Beyoncé leave Jay-Z when she found out the dirt he did? No...she had her little sister *Bruce Lee* his ass in that elevator...but she ain't leave him."

"Ain't the same thing," Corey said. "Beyoncé has her own money."

"True. But how many niggas she gon' meet that's got *Jay-Z* money?"

"Not many," Corey conceded. "He's in the Top 10 richest black people in America."

"Exactly! Beyoncé's with a brotha who's got more in the bank than her. She doesn't have to worry about her man taking all of her money like Mary J. Blige's husband did her."

"What's your point?"

"My point is, Rene can take half of everything you own, but she'd spend the rest of her life not trusting the dude she hooks up with after you. You know why?"

"Why?"

"Because nine times out of ten, he ain't gon' have a fraction of what she has." Wayne elbowed Corey's shoulder. "You're an eight figure nigga who gave her a lifestyle that only an eight figure nigga can provide. You think she's going to be satisfied with a dude making forty thousand a year working at UPS? Dog, the first time that nigga says, *'Bae, I'ma be short on the light bill this month'*, she's gon' kick his ass out the house and start over. No woman pushing forty years old wanna keep having to start over."

"If a UPS brotha makes her happy—"

"Bullshit! Rene is mad...she ain't stupid. You think she wants to put all that time and effort into yo' black ass so another woman can reap the rewards? Hell no!" Wayne slapped Corey on the leg. "Cheer up, dog. She's just makin' you sweat. Give her a few weeks, she'll get over it. In the meantime, just give her whatever she wants."

"I can't."

"You can't *what*?"

"I can't give her what she wants."

Wayne brought the golf cart to a stop alongside the first hole on the golf course. He looked at Corey and said, "Dog, you've got enough money to buy damn near anything you want. Why can't you give the woman what she wants?"

Corey pulled a cigar out of his pocket and lit it. He puffed so hard that his head became engulfed in a cloud of smoke. When the smoke dissipated his face emerged.

"Yo ass always tryin' to look important," Wayne teased. "Answer the question. Why can't you give Rene what she wants to shut her up?"

Corey removed the cigar from his mouth and looked at his best friend. His bottom lip quivered and his hand shook. Eventually the words spilled from his mouth.

"What she wants I can't buy."

"Nigga everything has a price."

"Dog," Corey said in the most serious tone he'd ever used when talking to Wayne, "Rene wants to fuck you."

CHAPTER EIGHT

"Nigga, what the hell you say?"

Corey looked his best friend in the eyes. He took another puff of his cigar and blew it out slowly. "You heard what I said, Wayne."

Wayne continued to stare at him as other golfers enjoyed their day, laughing, blasting shots into the greens, oblivious to the fact that one of their own was losing his grip on everything he held dear.

Wayne planted his club in the grass and leaned on it. That didn't help. He still felt like he was about to fall over. He shook his head as he headed to their golf cart, which, thankfully, was parked beneath a beautiful oak tree. Corey followed him into the shade, and both men took a seat.

Wayne sat behind the wheel, but he didn't start the vehicle. After a few moments, he turned and looked Corey in the eyes again.

"Is this some kind of joke or something?"

Corey shook his head slowly. "She dead serious."

Wayne's brow furrowed. He reached and rubbed his forehead. "What the... Dog, why the hell would your wife want to have sex with me? I can't even believe you right now."

Corey took another drag from his cigar. He held the smoke for a few seconds before blowing it out. "Rene says she wants to have a threesome. She said if I watch her fuck another man, it'll get me back for what I did to her – what I *been* doing to her."

Wayne shook his head. "That don't even sound like Rene."

"Who you telling?"

"And how the hell I get into it?"

Corey sighed. "She picked you."

Wayne's eyes widened as he watched him.

Corey told him, "She said since we're best friends, you should be the one to do it."

"To be in your threesome?"

"She said I should have to watch my best friend have sex with her. She didn't say it like that, though. She said some real nasty shit. I swear to God I'ma throw up again if I keep thinking about it; what she said she wanted to do... to you."

Wayne's mouth fell open. "But why *me*?"

"Dammit, man, I don't know! I don't want that shit to happen at all! *Who* it happens with ain't the biggest problem."

Wayne noticed his irritation, but he was having as hard a time wrapping his mind around it. "Are you sure she's serious?"

After another drag, Corey said, "Yeah. I think so. She said if I don't agree to it, she'll divorce me for cheating. She'll take as much of our assets as she can, she'll get custody of CJ, and I'll have to see my son on the weekends – every *other* weekend. Put me on child support and shit."

The thought of not seeing CJ every single day made Corey's eyes water. He didn't attempt to hide his emotions from his friend. "She knows she can't completely ruin me," he said. "She just wants to hurt me. She knows I'd do anything to keep my life together; my family, everything the way it is."

Corey wiped the tears from his eye, and then they shone red with anger. "She got somebody to record me and Jennifer."

Wayne didn't think this conversation could get any more bizarre, but that bit of news made his eyes flash open again. "Recorded y'all what, *fucking*?"

Corey nodded. "She sent me a video. Perfect quality. They recorded it in my office." His voice grumbled when he said, "Some motherfucker got in my office and put a camera in there – sent the video to Rene."

"Aww, damn, man." Wayne couldn't have been more shocked. "Who coulda did that?"

"I was thinking the cleaning crew," Corey said. "They're the only ones who have access to my office when I'm not there. If Rene got in touch with one of them and offered to pay 'em, they'd do it. They don't make nothing, but ten dollars an hour. Who knows how much Rene paid."

"Dog, this is crazy. How the hell did your slick ass let Rene one-up you like that?"

Corey grimaced. "I don't know for sure if that's how it happened. Maybe she didn't have nothing to do with it. Maybe someone sent her the video anonymously, and she's just running with it."

"Who would do that?"

"I can't figure it out," Corey said, shaking his head. "Ain't like Rene will tell me."

"Either way, she got you," Wayne decided. "No matter how she got the video, she got you."

"Yeah," Corey breathed. "And I just had a meeting with a CEO last week. He wants me to provide security for *all* of his restaurants. Got like twenty of them. I'm talking a multi-million dollar deal. But he's a hardcore Christian, and he won't do business with me if he finds out I'm going through a divorce."

"He said that?"

Corey nodded. "In so many words."

"So you feel like you gotta give Rene what she wants..."

"Not just to save that deal," Corey said. "To save *everything*."

"Well, you can count me out," Wayne said. "You and Rene are like family. I don't want no parts of that. But as far as paying you back with a threesome, I'd say that ain't a bad deal."

"The hell it ain't," Corey said, scowling.

"Bruh, think about it for a second. After all the whoring your ass been doing, she just wants to sleep with another man *one time*. She don't even wanna do it behind your back. She wants you to be there to give your consent – and *participate*. To save your marriage and everything you have, it's not a bad deal, just some kinky sex. Maybe you can talk her into bringing in a female instead."

Corey gave that some thought and then said, "That ain't happening. She wants me to be jealous, to feel what she's feeling. She wants me to watch a man have sex with her, just like she watched me and Jennifer have sex."

Wayne considered that and said, "That's deep, bruh. Well, however it goes down, y'all gotta leave me out of it.

Maybe once you tell her I ain't interested, she'll drop the whole thing."

Corey doubted that, but he said, "You think so?"

Wayne shrugged. "Can't have a threesome if the third party ain't in it."

Corey sighed. "Yeah. But what if she go find some other nigga I don't even know?"

"You think you'd feel better if it's somebody you know?"

"Man, I don't know what I think," Corey said, palming his face. "I'm still stuck on not wanting it to happen at all."

"I hope it doesn't happen," Wayne said seriously. "But you might wanna start warming up to the idea. If everything you're telling me is true, then you're gonna have to watch a man have sex with your wife, like it or not. But look on the bright side," he reached to pat his friend on the back. "It ain't like you gon' be sitting there getting cuckolded. You'll be having sex with her too."

"Thanks for finding a bright side," Corey groaned sarcastically.

"No problem, my nigga. That's what friends are for." Wayne tried to hold back his chuckles, but he failed.

When Corey got home, he hoped to avoid his wife, but Rene was waiting for him in the kitchen. She locked eyes with him and held the gaze, while CJ jumped from his seat and rushed to greet his father.

"Daddy!"

Corey had only been gone for a few hours. Rene was annoyed by CJ's unconditional love for the man of the house, but she knew it was wrong to feel that way. As far as their son knew, Corey was the same awesome father he'd always been. Even though Rene knew different, she would never attempt to taint CJ's perceptions of his dad.

"Hey, Lil Man!"

Corey lifted the boy and hugged him tightly. He locked eyes with Rene again over CJ's shoulder. She hadn't paid him much attention in the past week, but he could tell she was ready to talk now. Rather than attempt to avoid the inevitable, Corey lowered his son and headed for the back door.

"I'm gonna go water the garden," he told them.

Rene rose to her feet, though her plate of spaghetti was mostly uneaten.

"I wanna go," CJ announced.

"No, you need to finish your lunch," Rene told him.

"But I wanna go with daddy," the boy protested. "You didn't finish *your* lunch."

Before Rene could put him in his place, Corey surprised her by backing her up.

"CJ, don't talk back to your mama. She told you to sit there and finish your lunch, and that's what you're gonna do. We'll be back in a second. Don't come outside right now – even if you finish before we're through talking."

The boy only pouted moderately as he returned to his meal. "Okay, daddy."

The Grand's garden was a beauty to behold. Corey remembered when Rene first broached the idea of creating it. He wasn't too fond of the plan initially, but he rented a

128

front end loader and cleared a 20 by 20 swath of land for her. He helped lay the ground cover before filling the hole with rich gardening soil.

Rene was excited when they brought the first batch of seedlings home. Corey had told her he was done with the project after supplying the soil, but he followed her outside and soon found himself on his hands and knees right beside her. Rene named their achievement the "Love Garden," long before the seedlings rooted and grew into the marvels they were today.

As beautiful and tranquil as their creation was, Corey felt no peace as he turned the faucet on and bent to retrieve the hose nozzle. He lit a cigarette before spraying the greenery with life-giving water. In his peripheral, he noticed Rene approach and stand beside him.

"You're smoking a lot," she noticed. "You plan on quitting again, or are you back to your old ways?"

"I'll quit again when my stress goes away," Corey replied. "But every time I think I'm okay, some more shit pops off."

"Maybe shit wouldn't pop off if you could get your dick to stop popping off."

Corey rolled his eyes and didn't respond to that.

"So, did you talk to him?" Rene asked.

Corey frowned and said, "Who?"

"You know who I'm talking about," Rene said, moving a hand to her hip. "You went out and played golf this morning. Are you going with someone different nowadays, or did you even play golf? Maybe you been using golf as an excuse to fuck more hoes."

"I haven't been lying to you about golf," Corey said, not trying to hide his irritation. "I talked to Wayne, and he said he ain't doing it."

Rene was incredulous. "*Really*?"

"Yes, really. What do you think, my best friend has been itching to get a piece of you?"

"No, I didn't say that. But I didn't think he'd reject me either."

"What?" Corey dropped the hose and stared at her. "Rene, what the hell. Is this – do you got a thing for Wayne or something? Is that why you picked him?"

"No. You know I don't."

"Well, you didn't just pull his name out of a hat. Why the hell you wanna bring him into our problems?"

"You brought him into our problems when you called his ass over here to say those panties belonged to someone he was screwing!" Rene barked, not backing down an inch.

"Asking him to lie for me is a hell of a lot different than asking him to fuck my wife," Corey countered.

"Oh, so now you admit he lied for you?"

"You know he lied for me! You got the video, right? And I'll tell you something," Corey said, advancing on her, "when I find out who took that video, I'ma kill they ass! That's an invasion of privacy! I doubt if you can even take that shit to court."

"Get your goddamned hand out of my face!"

Corey didn't realize he had a finger in her face until she slapped his hand away. He took a few steps back and tried to get his temper under control.

"You know what," he said, "it don't matter if you do have proof. Wayne said he's not doing it, so it ain't happening. But even if he had agreed, Rene, it *still* wouldn't happen. I'm not having a threesome with you. You're my wife! I'm not down with none of that freaky shit."

Rene's eyes widened. "Oh, I know you didn't fix your lips to say that! Since when is a *whore* not down with some freaky shit?"

"I ain't no whore."

"Yeah, you are. You're a *man whore!*"

"Say what you want? It don't even matter at this point. The bottom line is we're not having no threesome. Get that out of your head. Anything else you want, I promise I will give it to you. But—"

"I told you what I want, Corey."

"Woman, why can't you see how stupid this is?"

"It's stupid? How is it stupid, Corey? You get to live your life any way you want to; gallivanting around the city like you're a goddamn single man, while I'm stuck here taking care of our home and our son. How do you think that makes me feel?" Rene's voice cracked towards the end of her sentence, and she hated it. She hated how her eyes filled with tears when she wanted to be strong and forceful.

Corey noticed her distress and lowered his voice. "Because it won't make it right," he argued. "If you get to sleep with someone else, it won't make it right."

"But *you* don't get to decide," Rene growled. The tears glistening on her cheeks didn't diminish her fortitude. "You don't get to have multiple affairs during our marriage without some kind of reaction from me. If I decide I want to experience what you've been enjoying, *that's my choice.* You're gonna give me what I want."

Corey noticed that was a statement, rather than a question. He shook his head. "No, Rene. I'm not. I'm not gonna watch you fuck another man – I don't care if it's Wayne or anyone else."

"You sure about that?"

"I'm one hundred percent positive. If you wanna take me to court because I won't agree to your threesome, go right ahead. Me and my lawyers will laugh you right out of the building."

She nodded. "I guess we'll see then, huh?"

"Yeah, Rene. I guess we'll see."

The couple stared each other down before Rene turned and headed back to the house. Winning the staring contest wasn't a huge triumph, but Corey was grasping at straws, so he claimed the victory for the home team. He smoked the rest of his cigarette and then smoked two more before following his wife inside.

The atmosphere at the Grand residence remained frigid for the next few days. Corey continued to sleep in the guest bedroom, though he was beginning to long for his wife's intimacy. They hadn't made love in nearly a month, ever since CJ spilled the beans about his father grabbing the babysitter's ass. Corey hoped Rene had changed her mind about the threesome when she didn't bring it up again on Monday, Tuesday or Wednesday. But on Thursday shit hit the fan once again.

Corey was enjoying a nice day at work until Carol walked into his office at lunchtime with disturbing news.

"There's an officer here to see you, Mr. Grand."

Corey looked up from the papers on his desk and frowned at her. "A *what*?"

"A police officer," his secretary clarified. "It's a constable. Shall I tell him you're unavailable?"

Corey continued to stare at her in shock. He knew a constable would only visit him in person to deliver news from a court. Was he being sued? Surely Rene hadn't...

The blood drained from his face, but due to his skin tone, Carol didn't notice. Corey barely managed to catch his breath in time to tell her, "No, uh, send him in."

Carol backed out of the room and was soon replaced with an officer in full uniform. No black man in America would've been comfortable with that sight, even if it was only a constable. The constable still had a gun and a set of handcuffs on his hip. Corey's legs felt weak as he rose to his feet, but he managed to walk across the room and meet his visitor halfway.

"Corey Grand?" the officer wanted to know.

"Yuh, yes. Yes, sir."

"May I see your ID, please?"

Corey swallowed as he reached for his back pocket. He withdrew his wallet and handed over his drivers' license. The constable made notations on a notepad before returning his license along with a folded stack of papers.

"Thank you very much," the stranger said before turning and exiting the room.

Corey expected some sort of explanation for what the papers entailed, but he was okay without it. He could read just fine. He returned to his desk and took a seat before examining the documents. Carol reappeared in his doorway, but Corey shooed her away with a wave of his hand.

"Not now. Close the door."

His secretary did as she was told.

Corey didn't need to read more than the first page of his summons before his blood began to boil. He took deep, slow breaths as he called his dear wife.

"Hello?"

"What the fuck, Rene? Really?"

"What's wrong, baby?"

"You know exactly what's wrong with me. You fucking had me served?"

"Oh, that."

"*Oh, that*? What the hell is wrong with you, woman?"

"This is how people get divorced, Corey, if you didn't know. You get served, you go to court, and you tell the judge why you decided to fuck everything moving while you were married to a faithful woman who bore you a son. None of this is out of the norm."

"You had to get me served *at my office*?"

"I gave them our home address and your work address. I didn't tell them to go to the office, but I don't see what difference that makes."

"What if I had been with a client?" Corey bellowed. "Do you have any idea what this could've cost me?"

"It's costing you a *marriage* and a *family*. That should be the most important thing you're worried about."

"Okay," Corey breathed. "Fine. So this is real, huh? We're really gonna do this..."

"I've been telling you the same thing for weeks," Rene stated. "You don't wanna give me what I want–"

"A *threesome*. That's what you're telling me you want?"

"You make it sound like I've been speaking French."

134

"And all of this will go away? You'll drop this whole divorce thing."

"Yes, dear. I told you that already."

Corey sighed. His office tilted and spun slowly around him. His heart shuddered as he leaned forward and rested his forehead on the divorce papers. "I just don't see how that's gonna make you feel any better," he bawled.

"It's not for you to decide, Corey. You do enough deciding. You keep making selfish-ass decisions, but I can't make one? I never get to do anything that's just for *me*? Why is that? Because you're a man? Only men get to experience life on the wild side? You're the only one who gets to explore your sexual fantasies?"

"I didn't even know this was a fantasy of yours."

"I didn't either. Just like I didn't know you had a thing for sucking whore's toes. But I'm through arguing about this. Either give me my threesome, or get ready for court."

"This some bullshit," Corey cried.

"No, Corey. You cheating on your wife of ten years and then copping an attitude 'cause she wants *one* random dick is some bullshit."

"Wayne already said he wouldn't do it."

"He'll do it if you tell him to. That Negro drove halfway across the city in the middle of the night to lie about some drawers for you."

"Goddammit, Rene," Corey moaned.

"Stop acting like I'm asking for something completely outrageous, Corey. It's a *threesome*. They happen all the time. Do you have any idea how many people in this city are having a threesome *at this very moment*? Maybe if you get off your high horse, you'll realize this is probably something you'll enjoy too. And considering what you've been up to, you're getting off pretty damn easy. Anyway, I gotta get some food off the stove. I'll see you when you get home."

"Rene, wait–"

"Bye, Corey," she said and disconnected.

Corey remained in the same position, with his head down on the desk, for several minutes after she hung up. When he finally summoned the strength to rise from his pit of despair, he bit the bullet and called his best friend. Wayne was at work, but he answered right away.

"What up, dog?"

Corey sighed. He stared straight ahead, his eyes glistening. "I know you said you wouldn't do it, but I'ma need you to have sex with my wife."

That statement sounded just as horrible out loud as it did in his head – even more so.

After a pause, Wayne said, "Say, man, I already told you I'm not–"

"I got served with divorce papers today," Corey told him. "Rene's gonna follow through with this unless you do it. I know you don't want to. Trust me, I don't want you to even more than you don't want to. But if this is what it takes to save my marriage, *my whole life*, then we gotta do it. I did her wrong, and I know it. And, like you said, this is an easy way to fix things, right?" He sniffled. "It's just some kinky sex, right?"

"I also told you I'm not down with that shit. I told you to find somebody else."

"Are you gonna make me *beg* you to have sex with my wife? Is that where this is going?"

"Naw, Corey. I don't want you to beg–"

"Then help a brother out," Corey pleaded. "If I can agree to this, then you should be able to."

"You agreed to it?"

"I haven't told her yet, but yeah. I have no choice. The only thing I ask is that you, I mean, you know…"

Wayne waited for him to finish the sentence and then said, "No, Corey. I have no idea what you're trying to say."

"Just…" Corey shook his head. He couldn't believe he was requesting this. "Be gentle with her," he said. "Can you promise me that?"

"Corey… What the hell, man? Y'all dead wrong for dragging me into this mess."

"Promise me," Corey breathed. "I know how weird this is – all of it, but I'll feel better if you promise."

"Shit. Alright, man. I promise. You, I mean… Damn, Corey. This shit is just… *damn*!"

CHAPTER NINE

Once Corey and Wayne discussed Rene's expectations, focusing on hitting a golf ball was harder than trying to play poker in the front yard in the midst of a tornado. It was the shortest golf outing they'd ever experienced. As they rode on the golf cart back to the clubhouse, Corey's facial expression morphed from pitiful to angry. Wayne looked like he was torn between sorrow and intrigue. Neither would come out and say it, but their body language suggested that they both knew their relationship would never be the same if they honored Rene's request.

Wayne pulled up to the clubhouse and parked the golf cart in the designated area. He wasn't sure what to say, but the silence was deafening and needed to be broken.

"Dog, are you sure there isn't another way to handle this?" Wayne asked.

Corey shook his head.

"I just think—"

"Let's just do this shit and get it over with," Corey cut him off. "I want you to come over to our house tomorrow night—around seven. We'll make plans for CJ to stay at a neighbor's house or somewhere else."

"Dog, I just think—"

Corey interrupted by raising his hand. "Here are the rules of engagement: you wear a condom."

"I can't believe we're having this discussion," Wayne mumbled.

"You don't smack her ass or any of that other shit you like to do," Corey continued.

"Dog, I don't—"

Corey held up his hand again. "Keep your dick away from my wife's face and asshole."

Wayne grabbed Corey's arm. "Dog, do you hear what you're saying? This shit you're talkin' is crazy."

Corey pulled away and got off the golf cart. He grabbed his golf bag and said one last thing to Wayne. "If you think the shit I'm talking is so crazy, why does your dick look like it's about to burst through your fuckin' pants?" Corey shook his head in disgust and headed toward the parking lot. Without looking back at Wayne he yelled. "Seven o'clock tomorrow night!"

Wayne waited until Corey turned the corner before he looked down at his crotch and saw the bulge in his pants. He shook his head in disbelief. When the images in his mind became too plentiful and the magnitude of their conversation became somewhat overwhelming, the golf cart steering wheel became a resting place for his forehead.

"I can't believe this is really going to happen."

Corey drove with as much enthusiasm as a death row inmate walking toward the electric chair. The pros and cons of honoring Rene's request—as they pertained to him—were understood: he'd give her the *fuck pass* she demanded and he'd get to keep the things that were most important to him: his child, his money, and his marriage. But what about the aftermath?

Corey grabbed his phone and pressed the speed dial.

"Hello," Rene said.

"Tomorrow night at seven o'clock," Corey blurted out. "Find some place for CJ to spend the night. Rene, this is the only time I'm going along with this shit so you can take it or leave it."

Corey could feel his heart rate quicken as the words spilled from his mouth. He wanted to reach out and corral them, force them back to whence they came. But herding cats would have proven to be an easier task.

Silence reigned for what seemed like minutes before Rene finally said, "Okay."

Frown lines appeared on Corey's forehead. His face scrunched to the point his eyebrows became a uni-brow. His top lip furled and the veins coursing through his forearms grew as large as the sewer pipes running underneath the street he drove on.

Words jostled in Corey's mouth, all clamoring to take their place in preparation for him to ask questions like: *'What the fuck you mean?'* and *'Why are you so eager to fuck my friend?'* But, before his lips could part and those words could see the light of day, the phone went dead.

While Corey sat there holding the phone wondering if the call dropped because the battery needed to be recharged, a smirk as wide as a flat screen television formed on Rene's face. The far off look on her face would have made the devil shiver. The caring gaze of a loving, soften spoken, faithful woman that vowed to always be true to her husband had been replaced with a stare so cold she could have been the spokesperson for the phrase: *hell hath no fury like a woman scorned.*

While Rene stewed, the stunned look on Corey's face was an indication that he was starting to remember just how shrewd and calculating his wife could be.

In 2004, with a freshly minted Wharton MBA in tow and dreams of conquering the business world, Rene boarded an airplane in Philadelphia, Pennsylvania bound for San Francisco, California. Awaiting her in the land of sunshine and palm trees was a Silicon Valley job in the Procurement Department of Lockheed Martin.

Within two years Rene was maneuvering through the procurement world like a twenty-year vet. Negotiating, disputing, and overseeing deals between the research and development giant and companies from all parts of the globe was a daily occurrence for her until she married Corey and decided to become a stay-at-home mother. The job may have been a thing of the past, but the skills that helped her flourish in it were always within reach if needed.

Rene didn't need to reach too deep into her bag of tricks to broker the *threesome* deal with her husband. In fact, she utilized a lesson she learned in a Negotiating 101 class to bring her negotiations with Corey to an abrupt end: In any negotiations, the party that speaks first after final positions have been taken, loses. The winning party should end discussions after receiving the desired answer. In other words—whenever you're arguing with someone and you get the answer you want, shut up. Rene employed that strategy when she said, *'Okay'*, and hung up.

Ain't no fun when the rabbit got the gun, Rene contemplated before going into CJ's room to tidy up and make an overnight bag to send with him the next day.

With the wind blowing through his window and pounding his face, Corey became more and more aware of just how deep he was inside of his wife's dog house. As he sat at a stoplight waiting for it to turn green he reflected on Rene's disposition and thought: *They say you can't turn a bad girl good, but once a good girl goes bad, she's gone forever.*

By nightfall, Saturday proved to be as devoid of warm and fuzzy feelings as the other days that comprised the week. Corey read CJ a bedtime story, but was overwhelmed with emotion when the child insisted he lie beside him for a while. It was an unusual request; so unusual that it felt like CJ could sense his parent's union was hanging from the thinnest of threads.

Corey snuggled alongside his son in the twin sized bed and watched CJ's eyelids droop a few times before finally slamming shut. Corey knew not to try to get up too soon or else he'd wake the boy and be ordered to stay there longer. While he watched CJ drift off to that place kids go to when exhaustion wins out, a line from a Tupac song came to

Corey's mind: *'Lately, I've been really wanting babies, so I can see a part of me that wasn't always shady.'*

"Leave it to Tupac to capture a brotha's emotions in a sentence," Corey mumbled in a tone so low it sounded like a hiss. With great care he eased out of CJ's bed and went into the guest bedroom.

Corey went through his nighttime cleanup routine and then climbed into bed. The ceiling seemed to lower to the point that Corey could see every crack and spot in it. Eyes heavy from the weight of life's stress closed slowly. The moment those portals to the world shut out all light, his thoughts ran wild like roaches when the lights go off.

Rene obviously wants to be with Wayne. And based on the way she won't let this go, I believe the thought has been percolating for a long time. I don't know how I'm going to deal with her or Wayne once this is all over. What if she appears to be enjoying having sex with him? What am I expected to do while she's sexing him? Sometimes Rene takes a long time to cum. What if he makes her cum fast? What does that say about me? Will that be some kind of sign that I haven't been hitting it right?

Corey pressed his lids tighter hoping it would make the thoughts dissipate, but they only got worse. *I told Wayne to keep his dick away from her mouth, but I know Rene likes to give head. What if she tries to go down on him? What if she starts moaning and acting ways I've never seen her act?* Corey's teeth gritted behind his pressed lips. *I can't believe I married a fucking freak. If she goes through with this, I swear I'm gon' fuck one of her friends. But if I do that and she finds out I'll be right back where I started—at risk of losing everything.*

Corey grabbed one of the two pillows his head was on and placed it over his face. He screamed as loud as he could into the pillow. The pillow muffled the sound, but did little to control his thoughts. He removed the pillow from over his face and took a deep breath.

There's no way Wayne and I will be able to get past this. When I look at him all I'll be able to see is him fucking my wife.

At that moment the scariest of all thoughts emerged in Corey's mind.

I've seen Wayne in the shower at the Country Club. It's not like I was trying to peek at him, but he turned toward me and I saw his dick. He's hung like a fucking horse.

Corey gripped the pillow and pressed it on his face again. An even louder scream was unleashed. Once he got those emotions out he removed the pillow and took more deep breaths. His mind was betraying him. If he put that pillow over his face a few more times he might not live to see Sunday.

Corey got out of bed and went into the bathroom to grab two Benadryl pills. His next stop was the liquor cabinet in his home office. If his mind wouldn't rest on its own he knew how to expedite the process. A glass of Paul Mason Apple Brandy was used to wash the pills down and ushered him off to sleep.

Rene's struggles with getting some shut eye were as real as Corey's. While studying the ceiling in the master bedroom her eyes were as wide as a car's headlights. Deep down she knew the ultimatum was wrong, but her heart was hardened. Love still lived there, but was real close to being evicted.

I can't believe he agreed to it. I'm not sure if I should be offended or excited. I'm ashamed to say, but I'm leaning toward excited. I've always been curious about Wayne. Regardless of how attractive he is or how successful he may be, for a man to be involved with as many attractive women as he's had on his arms, he must be good in bed.

Rene's hand slid under the blanket and in between her legs.

I remember watching him dance at that Christmas party last year. A man with that much rhythm has to have a good stroke. Corey has absolutely no rhythm and it shows in his stroke.

Rene's finger seemed to come alive. It slithered inside of her hole and burrowed deep. Her eyes closed and a husky grunt escaped her mouth as she slid her moist finger out and the tip of her finger pressed firmly against her throbbing clitoris.

I've seen his dick print. He's gotta be eight inches easy. It looked like a sock in his pants.

Suppressed fantasies were awakened. Thoughts of wrapping her full lips around his swollen head made her nipples so hard they hurt. Her index finger was now moving with the speed of a jackhammer. In and out, non-stop. She could hear the juice in her vagina slosh.

It's been so long since I've had an orgasm without having to rub myself during sex. I know Wayne could make me cum.

"Wayne," she moaned. Her toes curled and a tidal wave of energy rose from her heels, up the back of her legs, spread to her butt and thighs and settled in her vagina. Her eyes rolled backward. "Ooh Wayne," she purred. "Wayne, I'm cu...cum...cummminnn..."

Rene's words were swept away in a sea of euphoria. Thoughts of Wayne pleasing her had the same efficacy as the pills and liquor Corey ingested. Her muscles relaxed. Those dreamy eyes of hers closed. A hissing sound oozed from her slightly parted lips. Sweet dreams awaited.

Wayne straddled his toilet. A lather of perspiration formed in the deep crease between his pecks and stretched all the way down to his six pack. His body quaked as he held all eight inches of his manhood in one hand and his cell phone in the other.

I know this ain't right, and I would never tell Corey this, but I bet Rene got some good pussy. Those legs. Those lips. That round ass. I'll bet she fucks like a porn star.

Wayne grunted and gripped his dick so tight that he could feel the veins that aligned the side of his pole throb.

I know Corey told me to stay away from her mouth, but I know those thick lips would feel good sliding up and down my dick.

Wayne grunted again.

All those times I caught you peeking. All those times you stared at me a second too long. All those flirty

146

comments you've made over the years. All that shit was real. You've been wanting this dick. You probably want this dick deep in that round ass.

Wayne's butt cheek clinched. Sweat trickled down his back and settled between the crack of his ass. He was stroking harder than ever before. His toes curled. Visions of Rene begging him with her eyes to go deeper brought him close to climax, but it was the thought of Corey watching him pound Rene's pussy that took him over the top.

"Fuck!" Wayne shouted. He angled his stiff dick toward the toilet just as a stream of sperm shot out.

Deep breaths continued to ooze from his mouth until eventually his body went limp. The cell phone, which to that point had been trapped in Wayne's left hand, fell to the floor. On the phone's screen was a photo of Rene looking voluptuous at last year's Christmas party.

Sunday's sun burst through Corey's window like it was eager to get the events of the day underway. His eyes fluttered before reluctantly opening just enough to take in the surroundings. His forearm shielded the rays as he rose like a boxer struggling to stand before being counted out.

A cup of coffee was what Corey's body yearned, but his momentum was halted when he heard a familiar voice in his living room. He stood in the doorway to his office and listened.

"Girl, you are lying to me," Jackie said.

"Shhh," Rene said. "Lower your voice. He's going to hear you."

"How do you expect me to lower my voice after what you just told me?" Jackie placed her hand over her mouth in disbelief before delving deeper into the discussion. "Let me make sure I heard you right. Corey...your selfish, self-centered, cheating, and never done nothing good but father that beautiful little boy in there, husband...is going to let you fuck his best friend?"

Rene nodded and sipped her coffee.

"So, he's just gone sit there with his dick in his hand while you fuck Wayne?"

"Well, technically it's supposed to be a threesome," Rene said. "That means he's supposed to be engaged in the sex too."

"Bitch, I don't need you to tell me how a threesome is supposed to go," Jackie said. "I know the difference between only having one dick at your disposal and two dicks staring you in the face. What I'm trying to figure out is what makes Corey think he gon' get a chance to stick his dick in anything." Jackie giggled. "Girl, I swear, I wish I could watch this shit. I'd pay money to see the look on Corey's face when Wayne whips out that anaconda sized dick he's packing."

"Would you calm down," Rene insisted.

"I'm sorry, I can't," Jackie said, waving her hand in the sky like she was in church hearing a sermon she agreed with. "I quit smoking, but Lord knows I wish I had a cigarette right now. Girl, I am officially living vicariously through you." Jackie reached over and touched Rene's leg. "Do me a favor."

"What?" Rene asked and took a sip.

"Take a picture of his dick."

Rene nearly spit out her coffee. "What?"

"Please...for me. I just gotta see it." Jackie closed her eyes and gnawed on her bottom lip. "Giiirrrrlll, do you remember we went to that pool party a few years ago, and Wayne's dick fell out of his swim trunks as he got out of the pool?"

Rene smiled. "Umm hmm," she murmured while sipping some more coffee.

"Girl, it was a thing of beauty," Jackie said. "To this day I believe his dick winked at me."

"Stop it," Rene said and chuckled.

"I'm serious. I think I came twice before he corralled that beast and tucked it back in." Jackie reached inside of her purse and pulled out a wallet. "Look, all I've got is a hundred dollars."

"Why are you pulling out money?"

"Bitch, I ain't playin'. I will pay you to take a picture of that niggas dick."

Rene started laughing.

"What...this ain't enough?" Jackie asked. "I can run to the ATM and get more."

Corey had heard enough. He cleared his throat and staggered into the living room on his way to the kitchen. He and Jackie locked eyes.

"Jackie," Corey grunted.

"Corey," Jackie replied. She put her money back inside of her purse and stood up. "Well, I'm gon' get going. I'll be back around five to get CJ."

"He'll be ready," Rene said and walked Jackie to the front door.

When the two ladies hugged Jackie whispered, "I can go to the ATM and get more money."

Rene stifled a laugh and pushed her messy friend out of the door. "Bye, Jackie."

Jackie bit her bottom lip, pumped her hips, and swatted the air like a woman being spanked during sex. She smiled at Rene and mouthed: *You better fuck his brains out.*

It took everything ounce of restraint Rene could muster to not burst into laughter, but she managed to stay calm and closed the front door. She leaned against the door and thought about Jackie's last naughty comment. She didn't reply out loud to her best friend's order to "Fuck his brains out", but the answer danced in Rene's head as she leaned against the front door and thought, *Trust me, I intend to.*

CHAPTER TEN

In the kitchen, Corey poured himself a cup of his wife's brew and took a seat at the table. He sipped it without sugar or cream and cursed himself when his taste buds came alive. Regardless of the problems they were currently experiencing, Rene still made the best coffee Corey ever tasted, even better than his secretary at work. He fixed cold eyes on his wife when she breezed into the kitchen, as cheery as a cherub.

Rene opened the refrigerator and asked him, "What do you want for breakfast?"

Corey glared at the back of her head until she looked back and asked him, "What's wrong, baby?"

"You think I didn't hear what you and Jackie were talking about?" he grumbled.

"Oh, that's just girl talk," Rene said, returning her attention to the fridge. "Bacon and eggs, or you want sausage?"

"I don't want anything – except to know what you're so damn happy about. Y'all in there yucking it up, like this is some fucking joke."

"Shhhh," Rene said as she removed a carton of eggs and placed them on the counter. "CJ's gonna be up at any minute."

Corey didn't think their son would rise this early on a Sunday morning unless one of them went to rouse him, but stranger things had happened. He lowered his voice and asked, "Do you think this is funny?"

Rene placed milk, butter and cream next to the eggs before closing the fridge. "I think I'm gonna make French toast," she announced.

Corey was growing irritated with the way she was avoiding his question, but at least the stove was facing him, so he could see her face while she prepared the meal.

"Why you not answering me?" he asked.

"I did," Rene replied. "I told you that was just girl talk."

"And this good mood you're in? What are you so giddy about?"

"You know why I'm in a good mood, Corey. Today's the big day. It's not okay for me to be excited?"

"You a little *too* excited," he said over his cup. "Like you've been wanting this for a long time."

"If two weeks is a long time, then yeah, I guess so. I've been wanting to get you back ever since CJ said you grabbed the babysitter's butt. At the time, I gave you the benefit of the doubt. But I told myself that if I caught you cheating on me *one more time*, I would get you back in the worst way. I didn't start thinking about what we're doing tonight until I got proof of what I knew all along."

"Proof? You talking about that video?"

Rene nodded as she cracked a couple of eggs in a bowl and whisked them together with milk, cream, vanilla, cinnamon and nutmeg. "That was the smoking gun that made everything fall into place," she told him.

"And I guess you won't tell me how you got that video?"

Rene shook her head but said, "Maybe tonight, after we take care of our business."

"You don't think this is gonna be weird at all?"

"Oh, I'm sure it will be, especially if you're still mad, and you decide to just stand there and watch me and Wayne do our thing."

That comment enraged Corey so quickly and so thoroughly, he wanted to jump up and throw his coffee in her face. He immediately felt ashamed of himself for thinking such a thing.

"That pisses you off, doesn't it?" Rene said, watching his eyes. "Good," she said, before he had time to reply. "Now you know how I felt every time you decided to commit adultery with one of your freaks. That feeling you have right now, think about all the times I was on the receiving end. Multiply it by ten, and you'll have some idea how I felt when I saw it with my own eyes. You *deserve* to watch me and Wayne do it. You know you do."

Her points were valid, but guilt had to wait in line behind the rest of Corey's emotions. "Tell me the truth," he said. "You been wanting to get with Wayne."

"If you're asking if I wanted to have an affair with him, no, I haven't. If you're asking if I think he's fine, sure. Any woman can see that. Why would I want to have my first – and probably last – threesome with someone I wasn't attracted to? That wouldn't make any sense."

Corey wanted to find fault in his wife's opinion that his best friend was fine, but he couldn't. Rene had plenty of friends he was attracted to. Even Jackie was beautiful, though he couldn't stand her ass at the moment.

Instead he said, "No one only has *one* threesome. You're liable to like it so much, you'll want to do it all the time. This shit could turn you into a freak."

"Watch your mouth," Rene said, peering down the hallway. "You know CJ doesn't always announce himself, especially if he hears us talking."

Corey checked the hallway as well and then turned back to her. "I didn't marry a freak," he said. "If you turn into someone I didn't marry, maybe I should be the one to..." He trailed off when he saw the look on his wife's face.

"I don't remember marrying a freak either," she said. "But I ended up with one, didn't I?"

Corey took a deep breath and let it out slowly. All of her arguments were on point. He felt like he was being drowned in a sea of his own sins. "Whatever," he said. "I'm just letting you know this ain't gonna become a part of our lives. You're gonna get your *one free pass*, and then we're going back to the way things were. You're not gonna ask for another threesome every time you get pissed at me."

"I didn't ask for this one because I was pissed at you for tracking mud through the house or leaving a pair of pants on the floor." Rene couldn't suppress her irritation as she glared at him. "I asked for this because you're a dirty dick bastard who needs to be taught a lesson."

Shocked, Corey was the one who looked back down the hallway to make sure their son wasn't approaching.

"And I'm not asking for another threesome if I catch you cheating again," Rene growled. "I'm gonna leave your sorry ass and take everything I have coming to me, like I should be doing right now. If I was you, I'd shut the hell up about it, before I change my mind and let my lawyers proceed with the divorce.

"You know you're getting off easy, and you need to start acting like it. Now I'm done talking about this. Do you want me to fix you something for breakfast or not?"

Corey took another deep breath and blew it hard from his nostrils. He couldn't figure out what was wrong with him. This threesome was a one-time thing, and it would probably be over in less than an hour. He had committed adultery more than a couple dozen times, and he certainly should be punished for it.

So why was it so hard for him to take his medicine? Was he really such an enormous asshole that he couldn't accept one sliver of the heartache he'd been putting his wife through?

"Can we, can we at least go through a couple of ground rules?" His shoulders slumped; his body language finally displaying signs of defeat.

"Not right now," Rene said, her beautiful smile back in place. "CJ's awake."

Corey frowned. He hadn't heard anything, but sure enough his pride and joy appeared a moment later. CJ wiped the sleep from his eyes as he entered the kitchen.

"Morning, Mommy."

"Good morning, handsome," Rene sang.

The boy's face lit up when he locked eyes with his father. "Good morning, Daddy!" He approached the table and threw his arms around his midsection. "Are you playing golf today?"

"No," Corey told him. "I played golf yesterday. I know I usually play on Sundays, but I'll be home with you guys today. Maybe you and me can play some golf together."

"Awesome!" CJ said, his face pressed against Corey's side. "And you can have breakfast with me and Mommy!"

At that moment, Corey wanted a cigarette more than the sustenance his body needed to survive, but he wrapped an arm around his son. CJ was the number one reason he agreed to his wife's demands. Every moment with him was precious.

"That's right, Lil Man. I'll be here to have breakfast with you and Mommy. I'll take some bacon to go with that French toast," he told Rene, "if you don't mind."

"Of course, dear," she said and went to retrieve it from the fridge.

After breakfast, the time crept by slowly as Corey counted down the hours to when his wife would boldly give herself to another man and force him to witness it. He was past the point of grief and acceptance, but jealousy held on tightly, pinching his psyche like a king crab.

He marveled at how Rene's mood seemed the exact opposite of his as she went about her daily routine. She straightened up the kitchen and busied herself with other chores, while Corey and CJ went to the backyard and practiced their putting on a stretch of turf Corey had installed on the opposite side of the garden.

Despite his turmoil, Corey found himself smiling and even laughing with his *mini-me* when CJ swung his club either too hard or too soft; rarely getting the ball in the hole. When CJ did manage to sink a five-foot putt, Corey cheered him on like he had won the Masters Tournament. He lifted

CJ into the air, while the boy squealed with delight, saying he was the next Tiger Woods.

"Tiger Woods, huh?" Corey replied. "That's cool. Just stay away from them white women and them pills."

CJ asked him, "What pills, Daddy?"

Corey grinned at his beautiful innocence. "Don't worry about it. You'll learn more about Mr. Woods when you get older."

At twelve-thirty, Corey and CJ contemplated their lunch plans. Rene surprised them by suggesting they all go to the Movie Tavern; where they could eat while watching the latest Pixar film. Initially, Corey wanted to hang back and let CJ and his mother have their time together, but the boy protested.

"Please come with us, Daddy! It won't be as much fun without you."

"Yeah, come with us, Corey," Rene said. "Why do you wanna be cooped up all day?"

Corey relented and ended up having a great time with his family. For the next few hours, everything felt so normal, it was almost possible to forget about the naughty deed that awaited them at seven p.m.

Almost, but not quite.

When they returned home at a quarter till four, Corey's apprehension grew steadily while he waited for Jackie to come and whisk CJ away, so the adults could have their *playtime.*

At four-thirty Rene began to pack their son's overnight bag in preparation for his sleepover with Jackie. Normally CJ would've protested being taken away from his doting parents, but he had been showered with their love from the moment he woke up that morning. For him, the sleepover was the icing on the cake of what had been an amazing day.

When Jackie rang the doorbell at five p.m., Corey made it to the living room first. He tried to suppress his rage when he opened the door, but memories of her comments that morning played in his mind like a CD on repeat.

I'd pay money to see the look on Corey's face when Wayne whips out that anaconda sized dick he's packing.

Take a picture of his dick.

Please... for me. I just gotta see it.

I will pay you to take a picture of that nigga's dick.

What makes Corey think he gon' get a chance to stick his dick in anything?

"Hey, Corey!" Jackie was all smiles as Corey invited her inside.

He grumbled something that sounded more like *Fuck you* than *Hello.*

"Where my friend at?" Jackie asked, either ignoring him or oblivious to his loathing for her.

"She's in CJ's room, getting him ready to go," Corey said.

Jackie stepped past him and continued down the hallway, as if she'd been given permission to stroll through his home. Corey followed her, fighting off a strong urge to grab a fistful of her hair and yank her back with all his might.

Good God, Corey thought, when he realized his hand was actually balled into a fist. He unclenched it and turned, heading back to the front room. *What the hell is wrong with me?* Corey had never been a violent person, but this was the second time today he was struck with a strong urge to harm someone – another woman, no less.

Rather than go into the living room, he veered towards the kitchen and exited through the back door. He knew CJ would want to say goodbye to him before he left, and Corey wanted to give him that opportunity. But he wouldn't be able to hide his fury with Rene and Jackie standing right there – snickering at him behind his back while he hugged his son.

Corey didn't bother heading to the garden before he whipped out his cigarettes. This was the fourth pack he'd purchased since his infidelities reignited his love affair with the cancer sticks. He even had an ashtray on the patio table now. It was filled with butts he was no longer trying to hide from his wife or his child.

While he smoked, Corey thought about all of the women he'd bedded since he stood before God and took Rene to be his lawfully wedded wife. He saw his mistresses' faces, their smooth, caramel skin, their luscious, dick-devouring lips.

All of his women were solid tens. Well, maybe Candace was a 9, and Samantha was an 8, but that was only because those girls didn't take care of their feet enough to make Corey want to suck their toes. But if he was only judging from their head to their ankles, every woman he had an affair with was a certified dime. As far as he knew, Rene was only aware of a few of them.

You know you deserve this for what you did to her, Corey told himself. *You got a good woman, a beautiful wife. Rene's just as fine as all of those skeezers you fucked, and she's definitely the most beautiful. She's wholesome, a great mother. She even put her career on the backburner, so you'd have time to build your empire. Stop acting like a pussy and take what's coming to you.*

Corey shook his head, trying to extinguish the voice, but his conscious kept talking.

You're a grown ass man. A motherfucking Grand! Grand's ain't never been no pussies, and you not gon' be the first one. In a couple of hours, you're gonna give your wife the pleasure she wants – the pleasure she deserves, and you not gon' care if Wayne is bigger, or if he makes her squeal louder than you do.

You already know Rene's gonna scream louder for Wayne. Even if he ain't putting it down that good, she'll do it to fuck with your head. If you let her get to you, you might as well sit in a corner and cry while Wayne's knocking down her walls, because you damn sure ain't a man no more. The fact that you came out here to avoid a couple of cackling hens says a lot about you!

With the matter settled, Corey put out his cigarette and went back inside in time to say goodbye to his son before CJ and Jackie took off. Corey did feel like Rene and Jackie were laughing at him behind his back while he spoke to CJ, but that was okay. Corey planned to give Rene more than she bargained for when they partook in their threesome.

He may not be packing like Wayne, but Corey had the advantage of knowing his wife's body to a T. By the time Wayne figured out what licks and strokes Rene liked, Corey would have her in the throes of a third orgasm.

Hopefully Rene would succumb to the pleasure and call it a night before Wayne had a chance to get his rocks off. Corey knew that was wishful thinking, but he needed something to believe in.

Rather than allow Rene to see how anxious he was after Jackie and CJ left, Corey retreated to the den and got caught up on a few MMA fights he had saved on his DVR. He wasn't really interested in any of the matches, but it felt good to watch sweaty men beat each other to a bloody pulp. Corey couldn't vent his own pent up aggression, so why not live vicariously through them?

At six o'clock he left the den and headed for the master bedroom. He noticed the fog of a recent shower wafting from the bathroom. He found Rene standing nude in their walk-in closet. She had already selected her outfit for the night. It was a sexy little number that featured a bodice, a G-string, and a garter belt to boot. Corey had seen her in the lingerie before. He had always thought it was her sexiest outfit. She noticed him approaching but paid him no mind as she sought out a pair of her sluttiest stilettos.

Corey stood in the doorway and watched her for a moment before saying, "You really going all out for this, huh?"

Rene turned to face him. Her nudity made her appear ten years younger. Corey noticed her kitty was completely shaved. Her breasts were surprisingly perky, her nipples standing erect because of the air conditioner.

"What'd you expect me to wear?" she asked, "an oversized tee-shirt with sweat pants?"

"Naw, I didn't say all that. I'm just tripping on how you want Wayne to see you; with your ass out and shit."

"He's gonna see more than that when I bend over and back it up on his dick," Rene replied.

Corey couldn't believe she looked him dead in the eyes as she said that. "You gotta talk like that?" he wondered. "You know you sound like a hoe, right?"

She responded, "This is the last time I'm gonna tell you: A hoe don't have the right to call someone else a hoe. If you weren't the hoe you are, we wouldn't be in this position."

Corey swallowed that down with little reaction, though beneath the surface he was starting to seethe again.

"Can we go over a few ground rules now?" he asked.

Rene placed her hands on her hips and half-sneered at him. "What ground rules, Corey?"

"Well, for one, anal is completely out of the question – *for Wayne*. If I decide to penetrate that hole, that's one thing. But he absolutely can't get nowhere near it."

Rene had allowed Corey to squeeze inside her little brown hole in the past, but she had already decided not to do so with Wayne. Corey's average-size dick had caused searing pain initially, until she learned how to relax those rarely used muscles. But she guessed Wayne had a good two inches on her husband, which would bring more girth too. She'd have to be a certified porn star to take that Mandigo in her ass.

"Fine," she said. "But if he can't do it, neither can you."

Corey frowned at her. "Are you serious?"

"Yes, I'm serious. This is *my* threesome. *My* fantasy. I'm not finna let you dictate how it goes."

Corey didn't really want to tap that hole tonight, so he decided to let it go. Wayne would never look at either of them the same if he and Corey double-penetrated the mother of his child.

"You can't suck his dick either," he announced.

Rene balked at that. "You can get the hell out of here with that one."

"What's the problem? You wanna suck Wayne's dick?"

"Stop acting like you don't know what a threesome is, Corey. If you take anal out of the equation, I only got two holes left for y'all; one in the front, and one in the back. If I'm not sucking dick, then y'all just taking turns having sex with me. That's not a threesome, that's running a train."

"Well, you can suck my dick while he's behind you," Corey offered.

"I'm sucking Wayne's dick tonight," Rene said definitively. "If you're lucky, I *might* suck yours too. You not finna wait till the last minute to start this bullshit, Corey. If you wanna cancel it altogether, we can. I'll let my lawyer know to proceed with the divorce."

"Man, what the... you ain't even trying to work with me."

"No, I'm not, because you're not in control this time! Don't come in here fucking with me while I'm trying to get dressed. You gon' end up stressing me out. *Move!*"

Rene advanced on him and pushed him out of the doorway. She slammed it closed in his face. Corey was so heated, he started to kick it down. But his cellphone began to vibrate in his pocket, followed by a ringtone he had reserved for his big dick best friend.

Corey's chest pounded as he stormed out of the room. He didn't answer until he reached the kitchen and was sure Rene couldn't hear him speaking.

"What's up?" Corey said as he stepped out of the back door and planted himself in what was becoming his favorite seat in the home.

"We still doing this?" Wayne asked. "You still want me to come over there?"

Corey pulled out a cigarette and lit it before responding. "Yeah, nigga. I told you to be here at seven o'clock."

"Yo', why you getting an attitude with me? I ain't the one who put me in this."

"Whatever, man. Just get your ass over here. We gon' do this shit, and then you can get the hell on."

Corey hung up on him.

Halfway across the city, Wayne stared at his phone in disbelief, and then a sinister grin parted his lips.

Fuck you, Corey. That's why I'm about to go balls deep in your wife.

Wayne chuckled as he returned his phone to his front pocket.

Wayne arrived at the Grand residence at seven as promised. Corey greeted him at the door, while their conquest awaited them in the second guest bedroom. It had already been decided the threesome wouldn't take place in the master bedroom or even in the one Corey had been using since Rene put him in the doghouse.

Wayne wore jeans with a form-fitting tee that showed off his above average pecs and shoulder muscles. Corey noted that he brought in the scent of expensive cologne as he crossed the threshold into the living room. Corey closed the door, and the two men turned to face each other. Wayne could see the signs of stress in his friend's features.

"Are you sure this is really what y'all want?" Wayne asked. "I can't lie; I'm feeling hella uncomfortable right now."

"It's happening," Corey spat. "Just come in here and hurry up and get it over with. Don't be prolonging this shit after Rene gets *hers*. This ain't about you. I don't even want you to enjoy it."

Wayne wasn't sure how he could not enjoy a fresh pussy that just happened to belong to one of the finest women he knew. Thankfully, Corey didn't expect him to respond to that.

The man of the house turned and headed down a darkened hallway. Over the years, Wayne had followed him down the same hall, but everything felt different now. The whole house had the aura of deception and rage, with an underlying tone of sexual tension.

Corey stopped at a room Wayne had never entered. He disappeared inside, but Wayne lingered in the doorway when he caught up with him. Inside the room, Rene sat on a king size bed. She wore a sexy black and red outfit that didn't have enough fabric to hide the swell of her bosoms, the thickness of her thighs or very much else. She locked eyes with Wayne, completely ignoring her husband, who had stepped to the opposite side of the bed.

Rene stood, slowly, dripping sexuality with each movement. Wayne swallowed hard as he watched her. She stepped to the center of the room, her eyes dark with desire. She wore her hair down, in loose curls. Her eyeliner was perfect, making her orbs appear large and innocent. The only other makeup she wore was a thin coat of red lipstick that matched her lingerie.

"Hi, Wayne," she breathed before performing a slow 180 degree turn that exposed her ass to him when she was done. Her heels sank into the plush carpet. She was facing her husband now, but when she asked, "Do you like it?" both men knew she was speaking to Wayne.

As hard as it was to take his eyes off her bare cheeks, Wayne looked past her and locked eyes with Corey. If Corey had a comment, he didn't bother voicing it. Rene looked over her shoulder, drawing Wayne's attention back to her.

"I asked if you like my ass."

Wayne's eyes left hers, and he stared at her backside unabashedly. He swallowed again before nodding.

"I can't hear you," Rene said. She grinned and shook her hips briskly, making her butt cheeks jiggle. She looked back at her husband and asked Wayne again, "Do you like my ass?" She narrowed her eyes and nearly laughed at the expression on Corey's face.

Behind her, Wayne said, "Ye...yeah. I do."

"Well come and grab it then," Rene said.

Wayne didn't move, but he licked his lips. He couldn't help it. Corey caught the move, and his jaws clenched. Rene chuckled as she watched her husband. She looked back at Wayne and saw that he still hadn't taken a step into the room.

She turned until she faced him fully. She told him, "This is gonna take all night, if you don't get a move on."

Rene stepped to Wayne so smoothly, it didn't appear that she was wearing heels. She didn't stop walking when she invaded his personal space, not until her breasts pressed against his massive torso. She looked up at him; admiring his height, dark skin, and strong jawline.

"Wrap your arms around me and grab my ass like you want it," Rene purred. She clutched his chin when his eyes swam in Corey's direction again. "No. Look me in the eyes and wrap your arms around me and grab my ass," she demanded.

Wayne sighed before complying with her request. His eyes remained locked on hers the whole time. Rene's body felt soft and supple in his strong embrace. Her perfume was tantalizing, but none of that felt as good as her ass in his hands. He squeezed her cheeks softly, tentatively, but Rene was having none of that.

"I said *grab it*. I know you're not a virgin. Grab it like you know what to do with it."

As Corey watched them interact, he began to wonder if he wasn't being cuckolded after all. Wayne gripped his wife's ass hard enough for his fingers to sink into her soft flesh.

"*Yeeeah*," Rene cooed in appreciation. "Yeah, Wayne. Just like that." She moaned softly as he began to caress her ass in addition to squeezing it. Her eyes closed, and her bottom lip disappeared inside her mouth. "*Yes, Wayne*," she breathed. "Yeah. I like that."

Behind them Corey's nostrils flared, but he remained mute. Rene paid him no mind as she reached between her legs, in search of the bulge she knew Wayne had hidden in his jeans. When she found it, her eyes flashed open.

"Damn," she said as she stroked his manhood through his pants. "Is this all for me?"

Thankfully that was a rhetorical question, because Wayne couldn't respond. Rene broke away from him, which pleased Corey immensely – until he realized his torture had only just begun.

Rene backed up to the bed and beckoned Wayne to come with her. He followed her stiffly, his erection growing steadily with each step. Rene took a seat on the bed and gripped the front of his pants when he was close enough. She pulled him between her legs. The bed frame was tall, but so was Wayne. From that position, his crotch was nearly level with her face.

Corey began to make his way around the side of the bed as she unbuckled his friend's pants. Wayne's eyes were glued squarely on hers now, as if he'd forgotten there was another person in the room. Corey had the surreal feeling of a peeping Tom as he watched his wife pull Wayne's zipper down and then peel his jeans past his hips. His dick pushed hard against his boxers, stretching the fabric like a tent, so she pulled those down too.

Corey knew how large his friend was in a flaccid state. Rene had seen the same thing when Wayne had a wardrobe malfunction at the pool. But nothing could prepare either one of them for the glory of Wayne's full erection.

Corey's eyes widened at the same pace as his wife's. He remembered how he'd implored his friend to, *Be gentle with her*. He now understood there was no chance of that happening. From the looks of it, Wayne would stretch his wife's walls to the point that Corey would drown the next time he slipped inside her – at least until her kitty snapped back in place.

Rene's mouth watered as she stared at the dark pole pointing at her nose. She took a deep breath and blew it out with a delightful, "*Whooo.*" She wrapped her hand around his erection. The first thing she noticed was that she couldn't close her hand completely, the way she could with Corey.

"*Damn, Wayne,*" she marveled, while staring at his manhood like it was a rare jewel. "I don't know if I can fit all of this in my mouth, but I'm gonna try."

Wayne didn't speak, but his dick jumped in response.

Rene took a deep breath before she softly kissed the tip. Wayne's dick pulsated again.

Corey stood five feet away now. He advanced quickly and said, "No!"

Rene looked up at him with enough malice in her eyes to turn him into a pillar of salt. But Corey's intrusion was not to stop the show. He reached into his pocket and produced a condom. He knew his friend was well-endowed, so he had purchased a box of Magnums.

Rene's eyes softened as she accepted the contraceptive. She ignored what looked like tears in Corey's eyes and tore the wrapper open with her teeth. Wayne and Corey silently watched her every move.

When she had the condom free of the wrapper, Rene used both hands to pull it over Wayne's swollen head, which looked as big and dark as a large plum. Corey hoped his wife would slide the contraceptive down his shaft with her hand, but no such luck. Rene leaned forward and hummed as she pushed the condom the rest of the way down with her mouth.

Wayne gasped as he shot a squirt of pre-cum. He looked over at Corey and shrugged, and then his large hand disappeared into the hair in the back of Rene's head. He gripped it tightly before urging her face forward, to see exactly how much she could take before her gag reflex kicked in. She surprised him by swallowing six of the eight inches.

CHAPTER ELEVEN

Dating back to their freshman year in college when Corey and Wayne first met on the yard at Clark Atlanta University, Wayne conceded the *Alpha* spot to Corey. If Corey said he wanted to go to a party, Wayne followed. When Corey wanted to fight another guy, Wayne went along without question. Whatever Corey wanted to do, Wayne acquiesced.

Wayne's willingness to play the Beta role, had nothing to do with physical traits—he'd always possessed a larger body frame than Corey so intimidation wasn't the reason. And it wasn't their looks. In fact, it was Wayne who'd been hounded by modeling agencies at the age of nineteen and urged to drop out of school and walk the runways.

Wayne even had Corey beat in book smarts too. It was Wayne who maintained a 3.8 GPA while Corey struggled to stay off of academic probation.

All of these things were proof that there was no cogent reason for Wayne to ever take a backseat to Corey in any arena. But, there was one intangible that Corey possessed and Wayne lacked—confidence.

Corey, who was by all accounts an attractive man, couldn't hold a physical candle to Wayne. However, he ran laps around his sidekick in the swag department.

When Wayne became nervous, Corey was the epitome of confidence. And not just any kind of confidence, we're talking supreme confidence. The kind of swag the rapper Notorious B.I.G. described when he said, *'Heartthrob never, black and ugly as ever; however, I stay Coogi down to the socks, rings and watch filled with rocks.'* That's the kind of confidence Corey possessed. It's the kind of confidence that makes a barely twenty-one year old man walk into his best friend's dorm room and announce, *'I'm dropping out of college and starting a security company.'*

But all that changed as they stood there in the Grand home. It wasn't anything that was said—just the look on Corey's face when he saw Wayne's penis. Neither man spoke, but they both new—there's a new sheriff in town.

Regardless of how often money is flaunted and braggadocios statements are tossed around, there remains one thing that men use against each other to claim superiority. It's the one thing money can't buy and all the chest beating in the world can't change—penis size.

That's right, the size of a man's dick remains the great equalizer amongst men. Primitive—yes. Immature—true. But in a land where women continue to insist that *size matters*, *he* with the biggest dick—regardless of bank account—will always have the last word.

There was no greater proof that the *size matters* rule exists than what was going down in the Grand household. The avarice that placed gaining and keeping wealth at the top of Corey's priority list was of no use as he watched Wayne's big dick sway like an elephant's trunk. While Rene struggled to secure the beast with her puffy lips, Wayne drove home his dominance by shooting a look at Corey that was devoid of compassion and filled with the glee of a man conquering his biggest rival.

This nigga lookin' at me like he's got a point to prove, Corey thought.

Wayne gripped a handful of Rene's mane and forced her to swallow until her eyes watered. As he and Corey engaged in a stare down fit for an old western movie, Wayne thought of a line from an LL Cool J song: *'Just because you're blessed with cash, doesn't mean your honey won't let me finesse that ass.'*

Rene gagged from his girth. Wayne showed pity and rocked back to allow his pole to slide out. A string of drool served as the tether between her lips and his head.

Wayne placed his hands on the side of Rene's head and forced her to look up at him. "You alright?" he asked.

Rene nodded and dabbed her eyes.

"Tell me what you want," Wayne said.

"What she wants is for you to let go of her fucking head!" Corey barked. "This ain't no damn low budget porn movie. Don't be talkin' to my wife like—"

Rene signaled for Corey to back off by lifting her hand. She never broke eye contact with Wayne. A dab of her nose with the back of her wrist and a clearing of her throat were her only actions before saying to Wayne in the sexiest voice she'd ever used, "I'm ready for you to fuck me until I cum."

Wayne curled his index finger and placed it underneath Rene's cheek; lifting her sex craved body until she stood in front of him.

"Take off your panties."

Rene wiggled her butt and the lace panties fell to the floor like Autumn leaves. Wayne managed to look away from

173

Rene's curves long enough to ask Corey, "You said this was a threesome, right? Well, how you gon' participate standing there fully dressed?"

Corey didn't like the condescending tone Wayne used, but if he was going to be emasculated he at least wanted to put up a fight. Standing there fully clothed while Rene and Wayne went at it like rabbits in heat wasn't his idea of fighting back.

Fuck this, Corey thought as he unbuckled his belt. His phone started buzzing just as he was about to drop his pants. He instinctively glanced at the screen. A frown emerged when he saw it was Jennifer's number. *Now this bitch wanna talk,* Corey thought and pressed the decline button sending the call to voicemail.

Wayne smirked as he watched the man whom he once considered to be the coolest guy in town, struggle to get his legs out of his pants. Rene, eager to get the sex underway, urged Wayne to refocus on her by gently placing her hand on his chest. When Wayne stared into Rene's eyes she bit her bottom lip and then mouthed: *Fuck me.*

With a slight bend of his knees, Wayne scooped Rene up into his arms. His huge hands gripped her butt cheeks like they were sponges. To ensure she didn't fall, Rene crossed her ankles behind his back.

"You want this dick?" Wayne asked and licked the tip of her nose.

"Yes. I want you to lay me down and give it to me."

"Trust me, I'm gon' give it to you," Wayne replied as he moved around to the side of the bed and pressed Rene's back against the wall, "but I'm not laying your fine ass down just yet." Wayne slid his arms between Rene's legs and his waist and lifted her body higher. Her ankles became uncrossed and she was suddenly solely reliant on him to keep her from falling. "Don't worry, I got you," Wayne whispered.

Wayne didn't have to lower her to make her feel him. Because of his height and the length of his dick, her vaginal lips were able to kiss his shaft without her having to move.

"He ever fucked you like this?" Wayne asked.

Rene shook her head.

Truth of the matter, she and Corey had tried this position, but he wasn't strong enough nor was his dick long enough to make it work.

"Well, I'm about to turn you on to something new," Wayne said, and hit her with his first pelvic thrust.

Rene gasped the way you'd imagine a woman would after having something the size of a toddler's arm shoved inside of her. The finger tips on her left hand lodged into the center of Wayne's back. Her right hand gripped the back of his head. She held on for dear life while he averaged a stroke per second for two straight minutes.

Rene's first moan rang out at the thirty second mark. Her whimper inspired Wayne to try even harder.

This ma'fucka really thinks he's a porn star, Corey thought as rage bubbled inside of him and trickled throughout his limbs.

One minute passed and Rene's body was beginning to talk back to her lover. Lustful pants spilled from her mouth. The sound of water sloshing between her thick thighs could be heard throughout the house. One minute and thirty seconds into her fantasy, Rene's toes curled. Her feet bowed and her legs shook.

"Yeah, it's comin' ain't it?" Wayne whispered.

It had been years since Rene and Corey's lovemaking was passionate enough to produce dirty talk. Two to three minutes of humping followed by a night full of snoring on his part was their new norm. She'd often watch him while he slept. Wondering if he put more effort into the concubines he kept for his pleasure.

Wayne's approach was different. He talked dirty to her—and she liked it. He told her what he intended to do rather than ask her if it was okay—and she liked it. Wayne didn't pretend this encounter was anything more than a good old fashion fuck—and she liked it.

Rene's *love* was seconds from coming down. The whites of her eyes were all that could be seen as she moaned.

"Let her go!" Corey shouted. "Somethin' ain't right!"

"Trust me, dog...everything is perfect. Ain't. That. Right?" Wayne asked Rene, making sure to go deep each time he pronounced a word.

Drool escaped the side of Rene's mouth. She bit her lip to keep the saliva trapped. Still, her eyes remained rolled in the back of her head.

"This how a woman looks when she gettin' that good dick," Wayne taunted. "You wouldn't know 'bout that...ole little dick ass nigga."

"Uhh!" Rene blurted out right as his strokes reached the two-minute mark. She lassoed Wayne's neck with her arms and lurched backward until her sweaty back was brushing against the wall. "I'm about to cum."

"You wanna cum on this big dick?" Wayne asked seconds before he leaned in and bit her bottom lip until he drew blood. He let go of her lip and latched on to one of her rock hard nipples like a breast feeding baby.

"Yes!" Rene shouted.

"Cum on this dick. You know you've been wanting it for years. Haven't you?"

It was the first time since Wayne entered her cavity that Rene looked over his shoulder at Corey. She could tell he wanted to hear the answer to that question as much as Wayne did. As her body bounced up and down on Wayne's pole and she watched her husband watch them, a decade's worth of animus rose within her like lava. All of his lies. All of his affairs. All of those nights when she cried herself to sleep. She wasn't to the point that love no longer lived in her heart, but at that moment—as she could feel her body succumbing to the curve of Wayne's thick dick—love for her husband was nowhere to be found.

"Yes!" Rene screamed out.

"Give it to me," Wayne demanded. The muscles in his back rolled like a tide. His hamstrings danced as he flexed. The dimples in his butt appeared as he put every ounce of energy he had into every deep, jackhammer style, stroke.

Rene dropped her left hand and held on for dear life with her right hand while she fondled her swollen clitoris.

"Uhh...uhhh...uhhhhhh!"

"Yeah, that's what I'm talkin' 'bout," Wayne said and smirked. "Cee, did you know your woman is a squirter?"

While Corey stood there, limp dick and all, wondering who this woman was masquerading as his wife, Wayne turned around without warning and placed Rene on the bed. He watched her squirm as bolts of pleasure shot through her arms and legs.

"Now that's an orgasm," Wayne said.

"That's enough," Corey said and pulled up his pants.

"Nawh nigga, this ain't enough," Wayne replied and turned Rene's limp body over. He grabbed her by the waist and forced her to get on her knees. Rene didn't put up a fight. Even if she wanted to her body wouldn't have cooperated. "Payback is a bitch, ain't it?"

Corey's face scrunched. "What the fuck you mean? You starting to sound like a bitch."

"Nawh, dog," Wayne replied as he entered Rene from the back, "I sound like a nigga who never forgot that his best friend fucked the only woman he every truly loved back when they were in college." Wayne smacked Rene's butt. "Is this how you fucked Sonya Lupo back when we were in college? Did you hit it doggy style like this?"

"Are you serious?" Corey asked, looking shocked.

"Oh, I'm dead serious," Wayne said and sneered when he saw Rene grip the sheets. "All these years you didn't think I knew what happened, but I did, I just decided to leave it alone. I saw her coming out of your dorm room that night. I was mad at her for cheating on me, but I hated you for doing that to me. I was s'posed to be your boy."

The hurt feelings roaming inside of Wayne's body morphed into anger. He gritted his teeth and pounded Rene so hard that sweat dripped from the bridge of his nose and landed on her back.

"Uhhh!" Rene called out. "Don't stop fucking me!"

"Here comes number two!" Wayne said as he watched Rene's back rise and her grip on the bed sheets become tighter. "Why you think I'm here, dog? Why you think it's so easy for me to fuck the shit out of your wife in front of you? It's because I've been wanting to get back at your ass for years." Wayne smacked Rene's butt again. "I just didn't realize how much I wanted to get back at you until I got deep...in...side...this...pussy!"

"Back up!" Corey ordered as he zipped his pants.

"Shiii, I'll back up when I'm ready to skeet on her ass."

"I said, back up."

"Hold up, dog," Wayne said. "I'm almost there." Wayne smacked Rene's butt again. "Ya see what happens when you're constantly fucking over people. That shit can come back and haunt you—like a nightmare. Today, I'm your fucking nightmare. Me and my big...long...black—"

"Nigga, I said back the fuck up!" Corey shouted and shoved the barrow of the baseball bat Rene kept for protection into Wayne's throat.

Corey's momentum forced Wayne to back up until his back hit the same spot on the wall where he had Rene.

"Corey stop!" Rene screamed.

"You better shut yo' ass up before I Barry Bonds yo' ass too!" Corey said, his free arm extended in her direction and his index finger shooting out at her like the tip of a spear. "Get out of here and go wash up...now!"

Rene didn't leave as she was told. Instead, she sat Indian style in the bed and hugged the pillow. "Don't hurt him," she pleaded.

Corey looked at Wayne and pointed the barrow inches away from Wayne's nose.

"I should bash your fuckin' head in. All this time you pretended like you didn't wanna sleep with my wife when you really wanted to get back at me."

Wayne stood there, dick dangling and his heart beating fast enough to burst through his chest. When he regained his composure enough to speak he swatted away the barrow of the bat and said, "If you were going to bash my head in you would've done it by now."

"Don't tempt me, nigga," Corey said.

"Do what you gotta do," Wayne said and brushed past Corey like he was an inanimate object. He walked over to his pile of clothes and put each item on. "You know what, Cee," Wayne said while putting on his pants, "you've hurt a lot of people over the years. You've hurt your wife. You've hurt other women." Wayne pulled his shirt over his head and yanked down on the bottom until it was as snug fitting as it was when he arrived. "And you've hurt me." Wayne grabbed one of his shoes and sat on the edge of the bed. Before he put on the shoe he looked up at Corey. "You were the only person who knew I was going to propose to Sonya." He chuckled and shook his head. "Hell, you came with me to the jewelry store to pick out the engagement ring."

"Wayne, that was over fifteen years ago," Corey said and lowered the bat until it rested against his own leg.

"One year. Ten years. Fifteen years. The shit still hurts. But I guess it doesn't bother the person who wasn't wounded." Wayne put on the first shoe and then looked at Corey before putting the second shoe on. "You had your pick of women—you fucked the chick I was going to propose to on the day I was going to propose to her." Wayne put on the shoe. His head shook while he stared at the floor. "I idolized your ass. You said and did everything I always wanted to say and do. I looked up to you so much that I figured losing my best friend over a chick that would fuck my best friend wasn't worth it." Wayne stood up. "All these years later, I finally realize that a *real* best friend would've kicked her scandalous ass out of his room."

"I'm sorry," Corey whispered.

"Too late for that playa," Wayne replied. He moved toward the entrance to the bedroom and pointed a finger at himself and then at Rene before saying, "Now you know what it means when they say: hurt people...hurt people."

Corey watched Wayne leave the room. He stood as stiff as a mannequin in that spot until he heard the front door open and close.

Like an oscillating fan, he turned and looked at Rene. She was still sitting in that crouched Indian style position, but she was now crying into the pillow she held and rocked back and forth.

It was the first time in years—maybe ever—that Corey genuinely felt her pain. His mind told him to go over, wrap his arms around her, but his ego wouldn't allow it.

Corey managed to ward off the tear that was threatening to spill from his eye. Any crying he did was going to happen in the dark of night where only the shadows that occupied the guest room where he slept could bare witness.

The barrow of the bat smacked the side of Corey's right thigh a few times before he tossed it on the floor. He unleashed a sigh and rubbed his hands across his emotionally drained face. He needed to get out of that room, but before he walked out he said, "I'm sorry for all the pain I've caused." Corey swiped away that rogue tear as it broke free from his lashes. "I'll run you some bath water."

CHAPTER TWELVE

Never did Rene imagine the simple act of standing up for herself would emasculate her husband so thoroughly he wouldn't be able to look her in the eyes for the next three days. In the aftermath, it was hard to accept the role she played in the fiasco and how much of the blame she could personally take on.

With the threesome she wanted, the threesome that never was, Corey and Wayne would ravish her, take her one at a time and simultaneously. In the days leading up to their freaky episode, Rene had perused porn sites on her tablet and made mental notes on the role she would play.

The women in the videos she watched were often treated with disrespect, but she knew that wouldn't be the case with her threesome. In her home, with her husband and his best friend, Rene knew she'd be the center of attention, like fresh lobster tails at a seafood buffet. She knew Wayne would try to outdo Corey, and in turn, Corey would crank up his performance a few notches.

Rene expected to bask in their affection and be rewarded with a sexual experience like nothing she'd ever dreamed of. She'd never had a dick in her mouth while another rock hard piece slammed in from behind. She wasn't always a fan of Corey coming in her face, but that night she would've allowed it. She imagined all three of them coming at the same time; with Corey painting her face and Wayne yanking his condom off in time to spray his load on her back.

She wanted to tap into Corey's jealousy, sure. But in the end, she thought things would end amicably. Corey would never want another man to please his wife, and he would change his behavior accordingly. Rene would've escaped the monotony of her stay-at-home-mom lifestyle, if just for a night, and have the memories of her threesome to warm her heart (and her panties) for years to come.

Instead, she got a shit storm of epic proportions that – because of the heightened sexuality and the fact that Wayne gave her what might have been the best orgasms *of her life* – couldn't have been more conflicting.

What Rene planned was naughty, taboo and possibly even immoral. But the rage Wayne brought to the table was an unexpected variable. Rene didn't think she should blame herself, because it was Corey, once again, who had destroyed a relationship with his wayward dick.

Rene thought Wayne should've ended their friendship years ago, when the offense initially occurred, but who was she to say how long a wronged man should let his grievances smolder and fester. She'd been doing the same thing herself; marinating her grief and anger for years.

In any event, the old adage *Revenge is a dish best served cold* had never been so poignant.

In the days following the threesome, which was truly more of a cuckold, Corey surprised his wife with a demure, doting nature. Gone was his confident, braggadocios swag. Gone was the way he commanded attention whenever he entered a room. Instead he inquired about Rene's wellbeing, as if she'd just returned home from a lengthy hospital stay. He tended to the household chores, even going as far as doing laundry and preparing meals.

Conversation between the man and woman of the house was nonexistent, other than the few words needed to get through the day. But Rene knew it was only a matter of time before they would have to decompress. There was no way they could continue as a married couple unless they cleared the air.

Their talk came a full week after Corey held a bat to Wayne's throat and demanded that he unhand his wife. Since then, Corey had not yet returned to the master bedroom. Rene awakened early on Sunday and was surprised to find the guest bedroom empty when she went to check on him. She found her husband outside watering their Love Garden. She was disheartened to see that Corey was still smoking, but when she approached him, she realized he had an eCig, rather than a Newport.

"When'd you get that?" she asked him, speaking as softly as the early birds chirping in the distance.

Corey stood wearing athletic shorts with a tee shirt. Rene had a robe pulled over her nightgown.

"The other day," he told her. "I never intended to pick up smoking again. It was, just something that happened, with the stress and all. I got this eCig to help wean me off tobacco."

"So you're feeling better now, no more stress?"

The sun was barely on the rise in the western horizon. Rene folded her arms over her chest to ward off the morning chill. She looked down and noticed her house shoes were getting damp from the dewy grass.

"I don't know if I'm feeling better," Corey said honestly. He hadn't looked her way since she joined him. "I know I don't wanna have a stroke, so I'm not buying any more cigarettes."

Rene was glad to hear that. It was comforting to know Corey wasn't so depressed he'd given up on his future.

"Do you, are we ever gonna talk about what happened?" she asked.

Corey hit his eCig, which made a light glow at the tip while he inhaled. He blew the vapors out and gently lowered the water hose nozzle to the ground, rather than drop it. When he turned and headed for the house, Rene took that to mean he was still avoiding the inevitable. But he approached the patio chairs and took a seat. After a few seconds, Rene followed suit.

She sat across from him, grateful that Corey had discarded all of the cigarette butts as well as the ashtray that had been on the table for the past month. He looked her in the eyes, and she noticed the dark bags and worry lines that hadn't been on his face before. He appeared to have aged ten years in the past seven days. Again Rene was struck with guilt for the role she played in his condition.

"What do you wanna talk about?" he finally asked.

"Um, about what happened," she repeated. "You haven't spoken to me since... You know."

"Since you declared your love for my best friend – my *former* best friend," he said, correcting himself.

"I never said I loved Wayne," she countered with a frown.

"You said you've always wanted to have sex with him."

Rene shook her head. "No. I didn't say that."

"The whole scene plays in my mind nonstop," Corey informed her. "I can tell you every word that was said while he was here."

Rene prayed he wouldn't do that. For once, her prayers were answered.

"Everything I did or said that night was to piss you off," she replied, which was only partially true. "I didn't know he was gonna start acting like that."

"You didn't have a problem with it at the time."

"I did when I realized he was serious about hurting you. That was never part of my plan. I can admit I wanted to make you jealous, but I had no idea Wayne was so angry with you. I never would've done it if I had known."

Corey half-sneered at her.

"I swear," Rene said. "Why would I want y'all to be fighting? That was supposed to be *my* fantasy night, not some goddamned bullfight."

Corey sighed and then said, "Well, it's over now. You got what you wanted. You made me look like a goddamned fool. You made me watch another man fuck your brains out. That part is what you wanted, right?"

Rene wasn't worried about CJ waking up that early, but she didn't want their conversation to be laced with profanity. "Yes. I mean, yeah, I guess I wanted those things.

But not to that extreme. What happened that night – that was *horrible*."

Corey nodded. "Now you see what happens when you invite another man into our bed."

Rene started to apologize again, but she frowned and shook her head. "Wait, I can admit things didn't go as I planned. But you can't negate the role you played in it."

"The role *I* played in it? What was my role, to stand there like a fool, while some nigga fucked my wife? I'm pretty sure I played my role exactly like you wanted."

"No, I mean all of your cheating that led to the threesome in the first place. And what you did to Wayne in college, if it's true, you know you were wrong for that. You never bothered to deny it, so I know it's true."

Corey hmphed in an attempt to blow her off.

"Really?" Rene said, her eyes widening. "You mean to tell me you went through all of that without taking a second to reevaluate yourself afterwards? That night wouldn't have gone like that if you didn't do your friend dirty. It wouldn't have happened at all if you didn't do me dirty to begin with."

"So, what am I supposed to say, Rene? You want me to apologize to that man after what he did to me – to *you*?"

"No, I didn't say that. Whatever happens between you and Wayne is between y'all. I'm saying you should take some time to reflect on why you keep having sex with all these women, thinking it's never gonna come back and hurt you. Because in the *real* world – the world most people live in – there's consequences when you do people wrong. I would feel a lot better right now if you accept those consequences, so we can move on."

"Are you saying it was all my fault? You and Wayne didn't do nothing wrong that night?"

"Of course Wayne did you wrong, baby. And I did you wrong too, by trying to make you jealous. But you're the one who did me and Wayne wrong in the first place."

"Alright. Fine, Rene." Corey took a few quick breaths, expelling them roughly through his nostrils. Rene noticed tears in his eyes when he said, "I'm sorry I cheated on you, and I'm sorry I fucked a whore Wayne was stupid enough to want to marry. Honestly I felt like I was doing him a favor, but—"

"No." Rene shook her head, refusing to let him off that easily. "A true friend would've told Wayne that his girlfriend was trying to hook up with him. Even if you couldn't help yourself, and you went ahead and did it, the least you could've done was warn him about her afterwards. Instead you kept it a secret, just like she did. If Wayne didn't catch you, he never would've known."

"*Alright,*" Corey said, still breathing roughly. He wiped his eyes before the tears had a chance to snake down his cheeks. "I did both of y'all wrong, and y'all got me back. I deserved it. Is that it? Is that what you wanna hear?"

Rene thought for a second and decided his apology was sufficient. "Yes, Corey. That's fine."

He took a drag of his eCig and blew out a plume of vapors, which was surprisingly similar to real smoke. "So what now?" he asked. "I guess we're supposed to make up and go on with our lives, like this never happened."

"I do want to make up," Rene said. "But I don't want to forget what happened. Even if I wanted to, I can't. I think we need to remember, because if we don't, things will never change."

"And that change all has to come from me?"

"You're the one who thinks it's cool to sleep around," Rene agreed. "You're the one who keeps letting your selfish decisions hurt people."

"And if I tell you I'll never do it again, you're gonna believe me, just like that?"

Rene reached across the table, hoping he'd give her his hand. Corey stared at her for a few seconds before he complied. It was the most physical contact they'd had since the threesome. Rene reached with her other hand and wrapped both around his. She squeezed comfortingly.

"Corey," she said, staring into his eyes. "I saw the pain you went through last week, and I see the pain in your eyes now. I honestly believe you've learned your lesson, and you will never cheat on me again. If you tell me so, yes, I will believe you."

Corey's chest shuddered. He sniffled. He didn't reach to wipe his tears this time. They spilled from his eyes like rain on a windowpane. He wrapped his other hand around hers. The gesture made Rene's eyes run like his.

"I promise I will never cheat on you again," he said.

Although his declaration should've been a given, Rene couldn't stop her face from crumpling as she accepted his heartfelt words. She stood at the same rate as him, and they came together on the side of the small table. They held each other, tightly, wholly. Neither of them could say how long they remained lost in each other's embrace before they reentered the house, arm in arm.

The Grand's reunification was not a simple thing, but time heals all wounds, even the ones that were so deep they pierced the soul.

They didn't talk about the threesome again. Rene doubted if they ever would or ever needed to. She knew how much it would hurt Corey to relive the memory, and she had never been the type of woman to harp on an issue that had been resolved. Corey promised he wouldn't cheat anymore, and she chose to believe he'd keep his word. Watching his every move, waiting for him to do her wrong again, would've been more of a punishment for her than him.

It didn't happen overnight, but over the next few weeks she took pride in her husband's ability to reclaim his rightful position as the man of the house. Corey threw himself into his work and continued to make strides there. His confidence did not desert him when he returned home each day and looked upon the love of his life.

Rene made him a special dinner every day, for a full month. She knelt before him and helped him take off his shoes and socks. She ran his bath water and offered to help scrub his back. She didn't invite him back to the master bedroom, but she was receptive when he exited the bathroom one night and lie beside her. Rene turned and draped an arm and leg over him, like the old days. Initially Corey stiffened beneath her touch, but in less than twenty minutes she heard him snoring lightly. She smiled and kissed his cheek, before succumbing to sleep herself.

They finally resumed their lovemaking four and a half weeks after the threesome. It was the first time Corey had pleased her since CJ saw him touch the babysitter's ass. Rene didn't think there was anything new about Corey's sex game, but that first night, in her opinion, was the most exquisite lovemaking they'd experienced since their honeymoon.

Corey was more attentive to her body than he'd ever been. More appreciative. He went down on her and remained there for the duration of four songs on Rene's slow jam CD. By the time he rose, his lips and cheeks glistening with her essence, Rene had climaxed two times. Corey gave her another earsplitting orgasm with his average-size dick, proving that length and width sometimes came secondary to the way you work it and the unadulterated love behind each stroke.

By mid-August the temperatures in Dallas were still on the rise. Rene looked forward to the respite of fall, but she enjoyed the summer days as well. She sat alone in a café on a particularly blistering Friday afternoon. She generally preferred the outside seating, but with the temperature hovering around the century mark, air conditioning was a must.

Rene had only ordered a strawberry lemonade, while she waited for her lunch date to arrive at the restaurant. When she noticed Jennifer breeze through the entrance, dressed like a diva who knew how to beat the heat, she stood and smiled and waved her over to her table. It wasn't the reaction she ever thought she'd have for one of Corey's mistresses, but after all they'd been through, Jennifer was no longer someone she considered an enemy. On the contrary, the babysitter with the pretty toes was more of an accomplice.

"*Hey!*" Jennifer's smile was bright and genuine as the women embraced. She planted a European style kiss on each of Rene's cheeks when they backed way. "Girl, it's hot as hell out here!" the younger woman announced.

"You're telling me," Rene said.

She returned to her seat, and her not-quite-friend sat as well. The two women stared and grinned at each other as their waitress approached with a menu in hand.

"Good afternoon," she said, placing a menu before the newcomer. "Would you like something to drink while you look over our specials – or do you know what you're having?"

"Oh, no, I've never been here before," Jennifer replied. She placed a new Birkin bag on the table as she got settled. She checked out Rene's drink and asked, "What's that you're having?"

"Strawberry lemonade."

"Does it come with alcohol?" Jennifer asked the server.

"Um, I don't think so," the girl said. "But I'm sure they can add a shot of whatever you like."

"Girl, you drinking this early, on a hot ass day like this?" Rene questioned.

"I'm not driving," Jennifer informed her. "Got dropped off by an Uber. I was gonna call them back when we leave, unless you have time to..."

Rene chuckled at the girl's propensity to get whatever she wanted, presumably from anyone. She said, "I can drop you off, if you're not that far."

"Not far at all," Jennifer said with a smirk. "You know what," she told the waitress, "I'll take a frozen margarita, if you have one. That should help me stay cool."

"Top shelf?" the waitress inquired.

"You know it," Jennifer said, as if the whole world should know she'd never settle for less.

"Okay, I'll be right back with that," the perky redhead said before leaving their table.

"So, how was France?" Rene asked when they were alone again.

Jennifer's smile spread ear-to-ear. "*Gorgeous*! Just like the pictures. Definitely not as hot as this hellhole. I don't even know why I came back to Dallas. I should move there permanently."

Rene grinned at that. She knew Jennifer didn't have the means to do that on her own, but a young, attractive woman like her would have no problem finding a man to fund the relocation.

"Thanks again for paying for my trip," Jennifer said. "You didn't have to do that."

"No, I told you I'd pay for that video," Rene said. She looked over at the bag Jennifer had placed on the table and said, "It looks like you got paid *twice*."

"I feel guilty about that," Jennifer said, though her smile didn't ebb at all.

"Why do you feel guilty?" Rene wondered. "I offered to pay you for setting Corey up, and he offered to pay you to keep quiet. You did both of those things. Why not get paid?"

"I don't know," the girl said with a shrug. "I know you think I'm a shiesty bitch—"

"I never said that."

"It's okay. You don't have to say it. I slept with your husband, so it's okay if you think that."

Rene looked around to see if any of the nearby patrons were eavesdropping, but Jennifer didn't appear to have any shame.

"I do have a heart," the mistress revealed. "To be honest, Miss Rene, I almost backed out."

That was news to Rene. "Really? When?"

"It was the night the whole thing was supposed to go down," Jennifer said. "I called Corey to–"

"Wait, you what?" Rene cut in, her eyes widening.

"I'm sorry, Miss Rene. Please don't take this the wrong way, but after everything that happened between me and Corey, the *affair*," she said, lowering her tone and her cheerful expression, "I'd be lying if I said I didn't have any feelings for him. I hope you're not mad at me."

Rene frowned at her puppy dog eyes, which probably reduced men to rubble on a regular basis. But then her expression softened. "No, I'm not mad at you," she told her. "What did Corey say when you called him?"

"He didn't answer," Jennifer said. "He never called me back, either, so I just said the hell with it. A couple of weeks later I got my bags delivered, and I haven't heard from him since."

Rene didn't know how to feel about Jennifer almost double-crossing her or about Corey sending gifts to a woman after he had *supposedly* learned his lesson from the threesome. She decided both of these things were non-consequential.

"So, how'd it go?" Jennifer asked. "Was it everything you hoped it would be? I mean, you paid me $10,000 to make that night happen. It better have been *explosive*!"

194

Rene chuckled, though Jennifer's comment made her guilt start to bubble up again. As slick as Corey had always been, he still had no idea Rene didn't simply catch him in the act and concoct the idea of a threesome. The threesome had been Rene's endgame the whole time, ever since CJ snitched on his father, and Rene finally had the name and phone number of one of Corey's girlfriends.

The first time she called Jennifer and questioned her about the affair, the mistress stood firm and denied everything. But when Rene propositioned her with cold, hard cash to not only sleep with Corey again, but to record it, Jennifer jumped on the offer like the multitude of hard dicks she'd encountered in her short lifetime. When Rene received the video evidence, all it took was a little finagling and a lot of bluffing before Corey caved, rather than risk a costly divorce.

"It didn't go like I planned," Rene told her, "but it sure as hell was explosive." She laughed and told her what transpired that night. When she was done speaking, Jennifer sat stunned, with her mouth hanging open.

"*Oh my God*! That's *crazy*!"

"Yeah," Rene said, nodding. "I never expected Wayne to go hard like that. I swear if I knew he hated Corey, I never would've picked him."

"But he's the one you always wanted to get with, right?"

"Yeah," Rene confirmed, "for the last five years."

"It sounds like he gave you a run for your money," Jennifer said, a wicked smile parting her lips. "For Corey to get that mad, he must've been all that and then some!"

"Uh, *yeah*," Rene said, with a satisfied sigh. "Wayne was way more than I bargained for."

195

"But you liked it?" Jennifer inquired.

Rene's face heated as she nodded. "I did. That man is packing, and he was stroking. To be honest, I'm glad him and Corey aren't friends anymore. I don't think I'd ever be able to see him again without getting wet."

"Oh snap!" Jennifer said, laughing. "So was it worth it, Miss Rene? Everything y'all been through, would you do it all again?"

Rene took a moment to consider that. The heartbreak of discovering Corey had cheated on her *again* hurt like hell. Conniving with the mistress was exciting, but the video Jennifer sent broke her heart into a million pieces, even though she was the one who requested it.

In retrospect, the way Wayne berated Corey was kinda funny, and the pipe game Wayne was laying down was *absolutely incredible*. Rene was now *almost* positive she had a faithful husband who would never cheat again.

"Yeah," she told Jennifer. "I wish Wayne hadn't dogged him out so bad, because I was crying by the time it was over. But I would do it all again. *Hopefully*, I'll never have to..."

"You never know," Jennifer said, one eyebrow raised.

"True that," Rene said and then lowered her gaze to the menu on the table. "So, what are you eating?"

"Depends. Who's paying?"

Rene laughed. "Have you ever paid for a meal?"

Jennifer's eyes narrowed as she gave that some thought. "Yeah, but it's been *years*."

"Then you already know who's paying."

"*Ooh! Goody!*" Jennifer said, lifting her menu. "Don't worry, Miss Rene. I'ma take it easy on you. I'll save my hardcore gouging for those cheating motherfuckers!"

Even though she was referring to men like Corey, Rene laughed.

EPILOGUE

The road to reconciliation for the Grand family was littered with potholes, but the *post-threesome life* they were living appeared to be hazard free.

Corey spent less time at the office and more time with Rene and CJ. Rene decided it was time for her to get a break too so she put CJ in a Summer Day Care program so she could have more time to herself.

"Mr. Grand!" Carol's voice blared through the intercom speaker.

"Yes."

"Mr. Cole is here to see you. Should I send him in?"

A smile as wide as the Grand Canyon grew on Corey's face. He rubbed his hands together and pressed the intercom button again. "Yes, Carol. Send him in."

Wilbur Cole was as tall as a Cypress and as thin as a rail. He was forty-two years old and still struggled with acne. He wore spectacles that could double as magnifying lenses, and the only thing more awkward than his gait was his posture. But he was the best attorney money could buy, and Corey would have rather cut off his right arm than lose him.

"Bring it to papa," Corey said with his arms extended and his fingers wiggling like a child clamoring for cookies.

"Alright, alright," Wilbur said as he entered the office and sat in the chair in front of Corey's desk. He opened his briefcase and pulled out a thick document. "You asked me to close the Espinoza deal and that's what I did." Wilbur tossed the signed contract on Corey's desk.

"Yes!" Corey shouted and lifted his arms like Ali after knocking out an opponent. "I knew you could do it."

"No, you didn't."

"You're right, I didn't," Corey conceded and flipped through the pages to ensure his new client signed. "I'm glad I decided not to come with you."

Wilbur shook his head as if he pitied Corey. "Man, you must be getting dementia because that ain't how I remember it. If memory serves me correctly, I'm the one who told you to let me handle it; you coming to the meeting while Espinoza was only sending his attorneys would make you look like a novice."

"Oh yeeeeaaah, it's coming back to me now," Corey said and opened a beautiful cherry wood humidor with his initials emblazoned on the top. "You've earned this," Corey said and tossed a cigar at Wilbur.

Wilbur wasn't the most athletic of fellows so he bobbled the cigar before managing to trap it against his thigh.

"That's a Cuban cigar, fool!"

"My bad," Wilbur said. "You caught me off guard." He held the cigar up to his eye level. "Hot damn. A real Cohiba Behike 52."

"Yep! You know how I do!" Corey stood up and walked around to the front of the table and sat on the edge. He extended his hand. "Thanks for closing the deal for me."

"No problem," Wilbur said. "So, now that you are about to be a few million richer, how are you going to celebrate?"

Corey glanced at his wrist watch. "You know what I'm gon' do?" he asked rhetorically. "I'm going to get my son and celebrate with him."

"Now that," Wilbur said as he uncoiled his lanky six-seven frame and stood up, "is the smartest thing I've heard you say in years."

The two men shook hands again and Wilbur turned and left the office. Corey walked around his desk and plopped down in his chair. He stared at the contract for a few moments and then pressed down on the intercom. "Carol!"

"Yes, sir."

"Contact the answering service, and tell them to answer our calls. Let the people in training and sales know that we're shutting it down for the day. I want you to go and enjoy your day."

"Yes, sir!" Carol replied with about as much enthusiasm as her rigid personality would allow to show. "And congratulations on the Espinoza deal."

"Thank you. If it weren't for you it wouldn't have happened. I got something I wanna give you next week. For now, get out of here and enjoy your day."

Corey sprang from his chair, unfastened his neck tie, and was out the door faster than he could say his own name. CJ's daycare was less than ten miles from his office, so by the time Corey's employees were made of aware of the *get lost* pass he'd issued and were getting in their cars, he was already pulling up in the daycare's driveway.

"Daddy!" CJ shouted when he saw Corey walk in. The boy hurdled one squatting kid and side-stepped the next before leaping into his father's arms. "You came to get me?"

"That's right. I left work early so I can hang out with you."

"I swear, I don't think I've ever seen a little boy light up at the sight of his dad the way this child does when he sees you," said Deidra Comeaux; a six-foot tall Amazon with skin as smooth as caramel, curves like Foxy Brown, and silky dreadlocks that hung down to the small of her back. The woman had a body that would turn a gay man straight and a scent so sweet she'd piss off a bed of roses.

Lord, you know I'm trying to do right. Please Lord keep this woman away from me, Corey thought.

"How are you doing Mr. Grand?" Deidra asked and gently placed her hand on the small of his back as she approached.

"Uhh, um, I'm...I'm good," Corey managed to get out.

He tried not to look, but she craned her neck, determined to make eye contact.

"I don't bite, Mr. Grand," she whispered. "Unless you ask me to," she whispered into his ear.

Lawwwwd, why hast thou forsaken me? You know I'm trying to do right...

"We've gotta go,' Corey said and spun on his heels. He had his forearm positioned underneath CJ's butt. The child held on to his dad's neck for dear life.

"Bye, CJ," Deidra said.

"Bye, Ms. Deidra!" CJ replied.

"Byyyyyeee, Mr. Grannnnnnd!" Deidra said and waved.

Corey threw up his hand and waved while walking out the door, but in his mind he was cursing her presence.

I rebuke you devil. You and that fine heffa you just sent my way.

Traffic was surprisingly thick on the drive home. Corey struggled to clear his thoughts of the flirtatious childcare provider.

She probably thinks I'm a pussy, Corey thought. He glanced back at CJ and said, "But she just don't know, son."

"Nope! She just don't know!" CJ repeated from the comfort of his car seat.

Corey chuckled and used the rearview mirror to see his son. "Do you even know what I'm talkin' 'bout?"

CJ shrugged and shook his head.

"Good!" Corey said and laughed out loud. He honked his horn at the slow moving car in front of him and looked back at CJ. "What you wanna eat, Lil Man?"

"I want ice cream!"

"Ice cream it is," Corey said and yanked the steering wheel.

There was a Baskin Robin ice cream parlor a few blocks from their house so that's where Corey headed.

"You know what kind you want?"

"Green!"

"You and that nasty mint," Corey said.

"I like it."

"I know you do." Corey whipped his sports car in the only open space he could find. He reached back and unbuckled CJ's car seat. "C'mon let's go get some ice cream."

The two Grand men exited the vehicle with scoops of ice cream on their minds; scoops that would surely be mush once exposed to the Texas heat.

"Where's the store, Daddy?"

"It's down there on the corner. We've got to walk to it because there are no parking spaces near it."

CJ ran a few paces ahead of his father—kicking every lose pebble he could spot. Corey watched with pride as his son made flush contact with every pebble in his path.

"Watch me, Daddy!" CJ reared back his foot and smacked the tiny rock like it was a soccer ball. "Did you see that, Daddy!"

Unfortunately, Corey didn't see the kick his son was so proud of because he'd stopped walking a few paces back. Something caught his eye and zapped his ability to move. Rene and Jennifer were at a table together at a diner next to the Baskin Robins ice cream store, and their body language and wide smiles suggested the interaction was friendly.

Corey held out his hand and gestured for CJ to come grab it. The child did as his father encouraged.

"What's wrong, Daddy? Why you stopped walkin'?"

Corey pulled CJ over next to him and took a step away from the window. "I need you stand right here next to me and be quiet."

"Okay," CJ said. "We gon' get ice cream?"

"Yes, son. Give me a second. Daddy is checkin' somethin' out."

Corey stared at Rene and Jennifer. He was hesitant to move because he thought Jennifer, who was facing the window, might see him. He watched closely—like a burglar waiting for a family to leave the home he was about to pilfer. It was in that frozen state he remained until the waiter approached their table and both ladies directed their attention to their menus.

"C'mon, Lil Man, let's go," Corey said and snatched CJ by the arm.

"Now we can get some ice cream?" CJ asked, while being dragged along the sidewalk.

"Yeah." Corey said and held open the door to Baskin Robins.

"Hey handsome," the cashier said to CJ. "What kind of ice cream do you want?"

"Green!"

"Give him a scoop of that mint green flavor, and put it in a cup. And give me a scoop of Pralines and Cream—you can put that in a cup too."

The young cashier returned moments later with both orders. Corey gave CJ his ice cream and held the door open for his son.

Jennifer and Rene laughed like two high school besties who hadn't seen each other in years. Their laughter grew so loud that a few times Rene had to cover her own mouth.

"Thank God," Jennifer said when she saw the waitress heading their way. "I'm starving."

"Me too."

"Where's our food?" Jennifer asked.

"I'm sorry, ma'am. Your food will be ready shortly." The woman turned her attention to Rene. "Ma'am, this is for you."

"Ice cream," Rene said. "I didn't order ice cream."

"I didn't know they sold ice cream here," Jennifer said.

"No ma'am, we don't," the woman replied and then directed her attention once again to Rene. "That ice cream came from next door. I was asked to give it to you."

"Who asked you to send this to me?"

The waitress looked around the diner. "It was a man," she mumbled. "He had a little boy...oh, there he is."

The woman's arm shot out like an arrow. Rene followed her pointed finger; turning around in her seat just enough to see where she was aiming.

"Oh, shit," Jennifer said.

Rene wanted to say something too, but she couldn't. *Guilt* had her by the throat. The cacophony of sounds that swirled in her ears were replaced by the echo of her pounding heart. The only thing scarier to her than being spotted with Jennifer was the passive-aggressive way Corey chose to let her know she'd been seen.

Rene's water filled eyes followed Corey as he walked past the diner's window. She started to run after him, but decided not to. There was nothing she could say that he'd believe. The only thing she could do was pray; pray that the revenge Corey would undoubtedly have waiting for her wouldn't be as cold as the revenge she'd served him.

BRIAN W. SMITH
& KEITH THOMAS WALKER

ABOUT THE AUTHORS

Brian W. Smith is the Bestselling Author of eighteen novels. His novels have appeared on multiple Bestsellers List to include: Dallas Morning News, Amazon, Target, and Black Expressions, just to name a few. He has been awarded the Male Author of the Year award from several literary organizations and his books have been nominated for other literary awards.

When Brian isn't writing novels and traveling across the country to meet with book clubs, appear at literary events, or to give speeches to writing groups, he serves as an Adjunct Professor of Creative Writing at two colleges in Dallas, Texas (Dallas County Community College and Collin County Community College).

Brian is a native of New Orleans, Louisiana and currently lives in McKinney, TX.

Keith Thomas Walker, known as the Master of Romantic Suspense and Urban Fiction, is the author of nearly two dozen novels, including *Life After, The Realest Ever,* the *Brick House* series and the *Finley High* series. Keith's books transcend all genres. He has published romance, urban fiction, mystery/thriller, teen/young adult, Christian, poetry and erotica. Originally from Fort Worth, he is a graduate of

Texas Wesleyan University. Keith has won or been nominated for numerous awards in the categories of "Best Male Author," "Best Romance," "Best Urban Fiction," "Best Young Adult Romance," and "Author of the Year," from several book clubs and organizations. Visit him at www.keithwalkerbooks.com.

www.ingramcontent.com/pod-product-compliance
Lightning Source LLC
Chambersburg PA
CBHW031945130726
47905CB00002BA/742